I KNEW BETTER THAN TO TRY PRYING THE RECEIVER FROM THE DEAD MAN'S GRIP

So I stepped gingerly around the desk, got down on my knees, and craned until my mouth approached the mouthpiece.

"Bernie," I croaked, "there's a corpse in my office."

"What? Sorry, Charlotte, it sounded as if you said there's a corpse in your office."

"I did say—gah."

Time passes, and so does rigor mortis. The chilly fingers of the dead man sagged, brushing my cheek.

"Listen, Charlotte, we've got an awfully bad connection, here..."

With a sound like the creaking timbers of some ghostly frigate, the dead man's head swivelled bonelessly.

"...but I just wanted you to know that..."

Full of regret, accusation, and stifled hate, his sightless eyes regarded me.

"...the check is in the mail," Bernie said, and hung up.

————————— ★ —————————

Also available from Worldwide Mystery by
MARY KITTREDGE

DEAD AND GONE
MURDER IN MENDOCINO

POISON PEN

MARY KITTREDGE

WORLDWIDE.

TORONTO • NEW YORK • LONDON
AMSTERDAM • PARIS • SYDNEY • HAMBURG
STOCKHOLM • ATHENS • TOKYO • MILAN
MADRID • WARSAW • BUDAPEST • AUCKLAND

POISON PEN

A Worldwide Mystery/July 1992

First published by Walker and Company.

ISBN 0-373-26099-7

This book is for Ruth Marie

ONE

Arriving at my office in New Haven that sunny morning, I at once discovered three unwelcome facts:

1) There was a dead man in my swivel chair,
2) There was blood on my new green desk-blotter, and
3) My telephone was ringing.

No one else was going to answer that telephone. I alone was the editor of *Pen and Pencil*, a 72-page monthly magazine devoted to advising and encouraging new writers while getting—as swiftly and efficiently as possible—their subscription money away from them.

Sadly at the moment I was also the magazine's art director, circulation manager, distribution coordinator, and general dogsbody, a state of affairs that left me little time for becoming in addition its impromptu medical officer.

Still, I laid my finger on the dead man's neck to make sure he was as long gone as I thought he was, whereupon he toppled sideways out of my chair, stiffly and without relinquishing his look of horrified surprise.

Under the circumstances I found that look understandable. Brains on a blotter, after all, are bound to create some sense of startlement, the more so if they are a person's own.

As the dead man went over he took with him my address-book, the desk lamp, a pile of unsolicited manuscripts whose return envelopes I had been tempted to steam free of their stamps—the few that had come equipped with return envelopes, never mind any question of grammar, spelling, punctuation, or the rudiments of English prose composition—and, of course, that ringing telephone, which he was clutching.

I knew better than to try prying the receiver from the dead man's grip, but the voice squawking out of it now belonged to my agent Bernie Holloway, and I needed to squawk back.

So I stepped gingerly around the desk, got down on my knees, and craned until my mouth approached the mouthpiece.

"Bernie," I croaked, "there's a corpse in my office."

"What? Sorry, Charlotte, it sounded as if you said there's a corpse in your office."

"I did say—gah."

Time passes, and so does rigor mortis. The chilly fingers of the dead man sagged, brushing my cheek.

"Listen, Charlotte, we've got an awfully bad connection here..."

With a sound like the creaking timbers of some ghostly frigate, the dead man's head swivelled bonelessly.

"...but I just wanted to let you know that..."

Full of regret, accusation, and stifled hate, his sightless eyes regarded me.

"...the check is in the mail," Bernie said, and hung up.

THE TRANSFORMATION of calories into words, of words into money, and of money into calories again are the three basic cycles in a freelance writer's metabolism.

Meanwhile checks from Bernie were always in the mail, the way fish were in the water and stars were in the sky: it was their natural habitat, and they were happy there.

I was not happy. When I die and St. Peter asks me what I've done, I will say that I lived in New Haven where I edited a magazine, and St. Peter will gaze down pityingly at me and slip me a Get Out of Jail Free card.

It occurred to me that I could haul Mister Dead Man back up into my swivel chair and prop him up behind my desk, and pretend for a while that he was the editor of *Pen and Pencil* magazine.

Even the hole in his head would look reasonable then, especially if I also propped all those unsolicited manuscripts in front of him.

But while I could imagine him blowing his brains out, and while I supposed I could even imagine him shooting himself in the back of the head to do it—the hole in the front of his head was either an exit wound or there was a 9-mm cannon around here somewhere—still, I couldn't imagine him shooting himself anywhere without any gun at all, and there wasn't one. Not in his hand. Not on my desk, or on the floor.

Suddenly I realized how silent a three-story brownstone rowhouse could be when only two people were in it and one of them had been murdered.

At least, I hoped only two people were in it. The offices of *Pen and Pencil* occupied the brownstone's attic, half of which had recently been finished off with smooth white wallboard, fluorescent lighting, bright new windows and freshly silvered radiators.

The rest of the attic consisted of storage cubicles, dark and cobwebby, reachable only by low passages along whose floors the building superintendent scattered mousetraps.

This however merely bred out the stupider mice; only rarely nowadays did I hear the unmistakable snick! of some throwback rodent on a suicide mission, having its foolish neck snapped over a crumb of stale cheese.

I heard that snick now, though: once, and then a lot more times.

Which meant that either mus musculus was back there diving headlong to death *en masse*, or someone trying to creep down the passageway toward me was getting mousetrapped for his trouble.

Unhappily, I remembered that none of the other tenants of the building would be in today, as last time I looked Memorial Day was still a legal excuse not to deliver writers' paychecks.

Nor would any of my own crew of typists be arriving to make personal phone calls, refurbish their nail polish, teach one another new dance steps, or perform any of the other duties so essential to the regular issuing of a monthly magazine.

Now I thought I would leave all these tasks to Mister Dead Man, as a creeping murderer could do him no further harm and neither could those terrible manuscripts.

What happened next I cannot report with any certainty. I do have a clear, vivid memory of a pair of red high-top sneakers with mousetraps dangling from their shoelaces. I can still hear the clackety sound those mousetraps made, chattering together as the sneakers pounced.

But where precisely they came from and how a pair of sneakers could even hold an ether-soaked rag, much less press it to my face...

Most puzzling of all was what any pair of sneakers wanted with a week's worth of *Pen and Pencil*'s unsolicited manuscripts.

I would have killed to get rid of them.

Still, when I woke up they were definitely gone.

"VROOM," Joey Rosen said about three hours later, lifting a pair of barbells so big just the sight of them made my arms hurt.

Joey's arms did not hurt. Due to the number of curls, lats, push-ups and other weight-bearing maneuvers he put them through every day, running a truck over Joey's arms might not make them hurt.

Running one over his legs was guaranteed not to hurt, because from the waist down Joey couldn't feel anything. Tumor surgery on his spinal cord a year earlier had taken care of that. It was why we were in

New Haven: so he could get the physical therapy he needed to do as much as possible with the body he had left.

Luckily, doing as much as possible came naturally to Joey. Sitting in his wheelchair now he was studying his Latin homework, listening to an Iron Maiden tape, and transforming his already bulging biceps into a substance just slightly harder than zirconium.

Meanwhile I lay on Helen Terrell's chintz sofa— away on a year's tour of Europe, my friend Helen had left her New Haven townhouse to my tender care—recovering as best I could from my bout of unscheduled general anesthesia.

My eyes felt as if they'd been cooked in a microwave oven, and every time I moved my head a pile of broken glass shifted from one cranial compartment to the other. I had cured my nausea by the simple method of upchucking everything I had ever eaten in my life, but the sensation that replaced it was no barrel of laughs either.

Also, I had been talking to the police, whom I had summoned by crawling down three flights of stairs, staggering drunkenly across a busy street, and falling head-first into a phone booth.

Once I got there of course I could not find a dime, although that didn't matter since I also could not get up off the floor of the phone booth. But by then someone else had called the police—not to report a murder, but to complain about the drunken lady making a spectacle of herself on a public street—and two escapees from a Deputy Dawg cartoon had arrived without delay and apprehended me.

At first the cops thought I needed to be delivered to the drunk tank. Then one of them noticed that I smelled like ether, and this convinced them that I needed to be arrested first as there is nothing like a good solid whiff of ether to make the cops think you are running an illegal drug factory down in the basement behind your washing-machine.

Next, while Deputy Dawg hunted through his pockets for his Miranda card, Quick-Draw McGraw noticed an important fact which was that I had an awful lot of blood all over me, and he did not understand how a person could get a lot of blood all over herself while talking on an office telephone, especially since my speech was still quite slurred and I was pronouncing it "offish."

Both of them, however, understood the phrase "dead guy"—I think they teach them that at policeman school—and finally they went upstairs and found him. Also they identified him, from the wallet in his pants pocket.

"So how *did* you get blood all over you?" Joey asked.

Once he'd learned the blood in question was not mine, he'd returned to his normal activities; being my adopted son had mellowed his outlook considerably over the past three years.

"I don't know, he must have dripped on me." I shuddered. Having already scrubbed with soap and a rough rag, I still found the thought of Brillo pads attractive.

"Probably," I said, "while I was talking to Bernie, that rat. See if I ever help him out when he finds a body in *his* office."

"Corpse blood, yechh," Joey said, his eyes shining, for like all teenage boys he adored such things. "Who was the guy?"

"Wesley Bell," I mumbled. "Just one of the magazine's contributors." Then I fell back on the sofa as the whole awful import of it hit me again.

Just Wesley Bell, that was all; just this year's winner of the William Trout Memorial Prize and the biggest thing to hit fiction publishing since F. Scott Fitzgerald.

Also, just the backbone of *Pen and Pencil* magazine.

I'd never met Bell, only carried on the sort of brisk shorthand correspondence that obtains between most writers and editors. But writing as he did—smoothly, swiftly, and most of all reliably—Wes had gradually taken over my pages. Now without him my upcoming issue was a cover, two letters to the editor, and the few scraps of ads I had managed to snag.

So far these consisted of a half-column of personals and *Make Big Money At Home* scams plus two boxed displays, one from a guy who couldn't write his way out of a two-foot closet but who was nevertheless eager to *Polish Your Novel!* into sure-fire publishability upon receipt of a hefty up-front fee, the other from a vanity press offering to put *Your Novel! Short Story! or Poems! into Print!* upon receipt of likewise.

"So how come somebody shot him?" Joey asked.

"Um, I don't know," I said distractedly, calculating in my head: sixty-eight text pages, minus say one-third art, a half-page of ads....

The result made me wish humbly that I had those unsolicited manuscripts back, because although Wesley Bell had been the kind of writer who express-mailed his stuff a day before deadline, so it would arrive in its flashy orange-and-blue package just when you were really dying for it, he'd also been the kind who when he said he would have something to you, he had something to you: on time, in shape.

Except this time. Six days past deadline and not a word from Bell. His answering machine and I were old chums. I'd been trying everything, even avoiding the office all day Saturday in hopes of not jinxing the mail slot.

Eyeing me narrowly, Joey lowered the barbells. "Charlotte," he said, "you've got that look on your face again."

"What look?" I replied a shade defensively. "I don't have any look."

"Yes, you do," he said, "and it's that snooping look. Not only that, but I'll bet we're broke again, aren't we?"

So much for trying to keep secrets from sixteen-year-olds, especially my sixteen-year-old. The truth was, without a next issue our bank account consisted of that check Bernie Holloway kept promising to pry out of my last freelance client, and since the client had recently relocated to a post office box in the Grand Caymans I was not really expecting a lot of very fast action on this. Besides, Bernie had a habit lately of promising the moon and delivering green cheese.

Pen and Pencil's corporate owners, on the other hand, paid well and on time, but only upon delivery. I sent them a stack of camera-ready layout sheets, they sent me a sum of spending-ready money, and it all worked out very well.

Except of course when instead of a smallish parcel full of Bell's flawless prose, I received a somewhat larger parcel with a hole the size of Rhode Island in its forehead.

"Aren't we?" Joey persisted.

"Let me put it this way," I told him. "In about ten minutes I'm going to be down at the Burger King flipping hamburgers, and you're going to be sitting on the corner of College and Chapel with a tin cup in front of you. Does that answer your question?"

Joey nodded thoughtfully. "How much do you figure I could make at that, anyway? Per hour, I mean."

"Not enough to pay the new doctor bills you're going to have if I ever catch you really doing it," I said, but it was too late; I could already see him storing the idea away for use the next time I balked on the topic of his allowance.

I sat up; the room only spun a quarter-turn, which I took as a good sign.

"Charlotte," Joey said warningly, but I wasn't listening.

If I could get those stolen manuscripts back I could make an issue of the magazine out of them. Not a great issue, maybe not even a good issue. Still, it would be a finished issue.

If I couldn't get them back, I would have to write half a dozen cheeringly encouraging, blithely numb-skull *Pen and Pencil* articles—all by Friday, all by myself and all on the same dizzy text: f u cn rd ths, u cn b a riter & mk bg $!!!

The very idea made me think yearningly of that ether-soaked rag. So I tottered to the telephone, un-der Joey's disapproving frown. Whoever had done this morning's deeds had to be some sort of cesspool-dwelling literary sludge lizard; after all, who else would even know where *Pen and Pencil*'s offices were?

Luckily, I had the world's foremost expert on scum-shrouded, methane-breathing hackwriters at my fin-gertips. In fact, Owen Strathmore was himself a member of the breed. I'd known Owen back when he was buying copies of *Gentleman's Quarterly*—the old leather-bound numbers with curly 'f's, steel engrav-ings and brown, embrittled pages—and copy-typing whole stories out of them, not even bothering to change the characters' names.

Now, if only I could *work* my fingertips.

"Here, let me do it." Joey wheeled over, reluc-tantly and as if this were all much against his better judgment. Moments later I had Owen on the line.

"Charlotte," he greeted me in a voice that was cu-riously minus its standard gale-force blowhardiness.

Owen was a hack, but he was a prosperous hack, and always prepared to share his latest triumphs just in case one had not heard: his just-finished short story, which with his connections was certain to win the whatzit prize; his new multiple-book contract for thus-and-so huge amount, reprint rights guaranteed for that other vast sum more, and of course the ever-possible film deal.

Life in fact was just ducky for Owen Strathmore lately, so much so that he seemed to have forgotten all those brittle steel engravings of flower-selling orphans and vitamin-deficient little match girls. Now, however, he seemed to be shivering.

"Listen," I began cautiously; Owen Strathmore shivering was like Mount Rushmore crumbling. "I happened to stop by the office this morning, and—"

"Right," he broke in, "I saw it on the noon news. I've got a call in to my lawyers right this minute."

"Really," I said, and paused. In my experience, the only thing likely to provoke a fit of nerves in Owen Strathmore was a world-wide scarcity of printer's ink.

"Charlotte," he entreated, "do you think that possibly you could come over here? I know," he added, "I haven't been the world's most supportive friend myself, but...."

At this I just stood there and gawped.

"...but," he continued helplessly, "I simply don't know who else to ask."

He stopped, and now I was certain I heard him sobbing.

"The thing is," he went on eventually, once he had gotten some control of himself again, "I'm going to be arrested for murder. I know I am. I'll tell you why when you get here, but—oh, Charlotte, do say that you will come."

OWEN STRATHMORE'S house was a massive red-brick Victorian pile on Prospect Street, twenty blocks out past the last Yale buildings and nearly within sight of the Eli Whitney homestead.

Here the maple trees were sedately shaking the wrinkles out of their damp, spring-green leaves. There were mailboxes on the corners and fresh laundry on the carousel-poles tucked discreetly into the side yards of the big, comfortable-looking houses, and men in their driveways were washing the cars they had backed out of their neat, well-organized garages.

Owen's cadaverous Volvo hunkered on the cracked patch of concrete outside his garage, not so he could wash it—the spray of a hose would likely collapse it into a heap of rusted metal flakes—but because the garage was packed to the rafters with books. His lawn was a solid wasteland of crabgrass and dandelions except near the foundations of his big old house, where the plantings were equally divided between burdock and pickerel-weed.

The slate crazy-paving of his front walk was an obstacle course of rolled, rubber-banded newspapers, for while he was not interested in what he called the dim doings of the locals, he never got around to cancelling the newsboy's deliveries. Making my way up the walk, I lifted the iron knocker on Owen's massive oak door, but before I could let it fall the door creaked open a crack and a pair of sharp little frightened eyes peered out.

The eyes belonged to Anna, the elderly woman who came in to "do for" Owen five days a week and with-

out whom he would surely have starved, or smothered in heaps of his own unwashed linen.

"Oh, Miss, I'm so glad you're here," Anna said,
reaching out with a hand that for all its bony with-
eredness was still extremely strong. "He's awful upset, Mister Strathmore is, he saw somethin' on the
television news. I don't know what's wrong with 'um
but he's up in the liberry and won't come out, how-
soever much I call." Fastening her claw on my sleeve,
she pulled me in.

The entry hall was dark as a spelunker's cave,
walled with high, heavy shelves stuffed so full they
seemed ready to topple together. Pamphlets and
broadsides, tracts and anthologies, chapbooks and
treatises, commonplaces and compendia were jammed
in any which way, their mouldering silence broken
only by the patter of Anna's house-slippers.

At the hall's end a light could be dimly glimpsed;
urging me toward it, Anna poured out a litany of
worry and complaint, her voice quavering like an old
record on an antique gramophone.

"I told him, Mister Strathmore, there ain't no point
in buryin' yourself, just 'cause you got bad news. I
yelled up the stairs, I said, Mister Strathmore, you
come on out of there now and let me fix you a nice hot
cuppa tea. I know he's there, Miss, rustling around
amongst them papers he sets so much store by, I can
hear him. Otherwise I might of thought he'd done
something awful to his self, but he's not typing either
and you know that's not like Mister Strathmore..."

"Thank you, Anna," I interrupted her firmly when
she had led me to the staircase curving up to Owen's

rooms. Just ahead a doorway led to Anna's kitchen, and I lingered in it a moment trying to gather in the room's cheer before consigning myself to the gloom above.

The isinglass window of the woodburning compartment in the massive, antediluvian gas stove flickered warmly; atop it, a kettle chuffed out comfortable little puffs of steam. The faded old linoleum glimmered and the faucets gleamed; the cracked, ancient countertops were spotless and the claw-footed porcelain sink had been Ajaxed to snowy whiteness.

A blue-checked oilcloth was spread on the wooden kitchen table, and over it all hung the smell of oranges and cloves. I longed to stay there, to somehow inveigle Owen from his den, but I knew better than to think that he would come.

Sadly, I regarded the staircase.

"It'll be all right, Anna," I promised, putting my foot on the bottom step.

"Oh, I do hope so, Miss," the bothered old party replied, and I thought that Owen was fortunate to have her; she seemed, in her dithering way, so truly concerned about him.

Now following my ascent her blue eyes grew round as two marbles, for whatever lay "above stairs," she had never been permitted to see it—or, apparently, to clean it. As I climbed, the atmosphere thickened: a dank miasma of unaired rooms, undrawn draperies, and fusty carpets.

At the top of the stairs I paused, peering to the right and to the left. In both directions the walls were packed to the lintels with acres of antique literature broken only by closed and silent doors.

From behind one door, however, I heard a faint rustling as of some small animal buried under a mountain of crumpled paper, struggling to get out.

On this door I knocked. "Owen? It's me, Charlotte." The rustling stopped.

I knocked again, harder. "You asked me to come. Well, I'm here, and whatever's worrying you we can talk it over together. I'm your friend, Owen, remember?"

Which, I thought irritably, is the only reason I put up with you. I tried the door. Locked.

"Owen," I said, rattling the knob impatiently. "Come on now, open up. I'm leaving if you don't."

At this, there was a creaking sound as of something very large being lifted from an old wooden chair. Steps shuffled slowly across the room, with a noise like a rake being dragged through snowdrifts of confetti. Finally came the rasp of an old lock unlocking.

"Good," I said, but a moment later I wasn't so sure, as there Owen stood, a big bald mountain of a man, haggard and red-eyed, wearing a lumberjack shirt and denim coveralls. In one hand he gripped a small pearl-handled derringer, in the other a fifth of Jack Daniels.

"Owen," I said hastily, as the little gun looked to be in good working order while Owen's aim at the moment most certainly did not, "whatever it is, it can't be as bad as you think."

Swaying, he appeared to consider this, but after a moment he ponderously shook his head.

"Oh, yes," he intoned, "it can."

MAROON VELVET DRAPERIES gathered thickly at the windows of Owen's long, low-ceilinged workroom; beneath the wads of crumpled paper littering the floor, old oriental rugs overlapped. At the room's center stood a massive oaken table and a ladder-backed chair with a sagging wicker seat. On the table squatted a battered old Underwood typewriter.

Stacked by the machine were about sixty pages of Owen's current novel: his morning's work, I presumed, since in order to finance his habit of buying old books he was required to produce a new one approximately every twenty minutes.

Luckily the sort of books Owen wrote could not suffer much from the breakneck speed at which he wrote them. *Exsanguinator #23* was yet another thrilling episode in the ongoing—some said interminable—saga of Thimon Gador, an enormously angry and singleminded twenty-first century gladiator who triumphed over villains human and alien alike by the simple method of letting all the blood out of them.

Describing fast new routes for the exiting of this blood plus new tools for piercing, slashing, or otherwise establishing the exits was Owen's main—some said only—creative task while writing *Exsanguinators*. He was, however, very good at it, and considering the events of the morning I now thought this boded rather ill.

"Doomed," he moaned, slamming his fist to his forehead. As this fist still clutched the little derringer, it seemed at the moment quite an accurate prediction.

"Owen," I told him pleasantly, sweeping a sheaf of yellowed papers from a dusty settee and stifling a sneeze as I sat down, "put that silly gun away right now and find me a drink, or I'll tell everyone your pen names. Your *other* pen names," I added darkly, since of course he wrote Thimon Gador and similar books under pseudonyms like Rod Thomas, Donald Savage, and Maximilian Brand. But bloody adventures were not Owen's only stock in trade; he also wrote romance. Ghastly, gaggingly sweet romance which like his other books went into dozens of reprintings.

Owen's face paled. "You wouldn't," he breathed, but he put down the weapon and hustled to the drinks cabinet nevertheless, and withdrew the fixings plus a covered ice-cube bucket.

"Here," he said, hastily thrusting a glass into my hand. "If anyone ever finds out I'm Gloriana Hodges-Burnett, I'll—"

"I know," I told him, "you'll be drummed out of the bodice-ripping business and have to start writing dragon fantasies instead."

To his credit, Owen shuddered. I took a swallow of my drink mixed just the way I like it: pour Scotch, insert ice. "Cut to the chase, Owen. What's got you in such an uproar that you'd actually call me up and ask for help?"

That, of course, had to be what he'd been about to do, as Owen never answered the phone at all unless he was on the point of dialing it himself. He dealt with people who telephoned him by letting his answering machine record his calls, then erasing the tape without listening to it.

But now that he had me here he was having second thoughts. His lips remained stubbornly clamped shut, so I tilted my glass over his *Exsanguinator* manuscript. "Speak, Owen, or the big guy drowns. I didn't come over for the coy treatment."

Owen would no more retype pages than Gador would take prisoners. "All right," he said hurriedly, "I'm in love with Corinna Bell. Now move that glass, for heaven's sake, and do stop laughing."

I wasn't laughing, just nearly exploding with the urge to fall down guffawing helplessly.

"Owen," I managed, "she's a little bit out of your weight division, isn't she?"

Imagine a cross between Ophelia and an Arthur Rackham fairy princess: masses of wavy red hair, skin pale as a skim of ice. Corinna Bell had big violet eyes, a sweetly startled look, and a slim graceful body nipped tinier at the middle by the kind of waist you really could put your two hands all the way around.

If you asked me she also had the kind of mind you could put your two hands all the way around, with plenty of room for a couple of bowling balls, besides. But then, I wasn't in love with her. On the contrary, in fact.

"Very funny," Owen said huffily, "but your lurid imaginings aren't in the slightest to the point. The point is, her husband was a cad. A brutal, sadistic little cad, and now he is dead."

"Extremely dead," I agreed solemnly as both Owen's Scotch and his concern began sinking in. This, I gathered, was the television news that had upset him so. Channel 8's crime-beat stringer must have fed Deputy Dawg an extra Milk-Bone to get it so fast.

"I don't suppose," I asked Owen, "you have any evidence of Bell's caddish behavior? Hard evidence, I mean. Photographs of bruises, say, or reports of medical examinations?"

Now that I knew Corinna was involved somehow, I wasn't taking anything for granted. From what I knew of her, she was entirely capable of lying. Like birds are capable of flight.

"Good God," said Owen, "of course not. She's a shy fragile bloom of a woman, Charlotte, she couldn't possibly expose—"

"Right," I said, swallowing a little more Scotch. I'd known Corinna Whitlock long before she met and married Wesley Bell, and while I knew she was just about as slender as steel cable, I knew she also possessed the same tensile strength—the kind that could wrap around the neck of Owen Strathmore and squeeze without the slightest difficulty.

"What," I asked him, "were you doing this morning? And who can say—under oath, by the way—you were doing it?"

Owen flushed. "No one," he replied, "that I'd care to ask." Determinedly, I stifled another giggle.

"Where?"

Owen caught my drift. He wasn't stupid, just in love, which under ordinary circumstances would have amounted to the same thing.

Only these weren't ordinary circumstances. "In room 723 at the Mayflower Hotel on Crown Street," he admitted grudgingly. "Really, Charlotte, I don't see why you have to—"

"Shut up. And while you shut up I'll take another drink." As he poured it, I bethought myself. "What makes you so sure anyone will care? Or even know about you and Corinna, for that matter?" This whole thing wasn't making much sense, so far. With his best-beloved's husband dead, he should be happy.

Owen flushed more deeply, harrumphing in discomfort as he handed me the refilled glass. "Well, the trouble is that in a chivalrous moment I seem to have written a rather indiscreet letter. One," he went on, "in which I proposed to free her of her difficulty."

"Good Lord. You told her you would kill him?"

Owen hung his head in reply.

"Maybe," I guessed, "even said how you might do it? Not," I added, "that you ever really would."

This last phrase I pronounced just questioningly enough. He might have, after all. Stranger things had happened. In fact, I hadn't quite yet heard him say he hadn't.

"Of course not, you know me better than that, Charlotte. My specialty is writing about a killer, not being one."

Well, no; probably not. Still—

"Corinna was here in New Haven with her husband, I gather?" Wesley himself having come on some as-yet unknown errand to the offices of *Pen and Pencil*—without, I noted, having phoned in advance.

He nodded. "She called last night to say she'd be here, and insisted I meet her even though we wouldn't have much time. I got to the hotel around nine-thirty this morning. She was already there, and she left at about eleven-thirty. She said she had to get back to their own hotel to meet him.''

"I see." Eleven-thirty was just about when I'd found Wes, which if one believed Corinna meant that his rigor mortis hadn't been departing, it had been arriving.

That pretty much ruled out Owen as a suspect, it seemed to me, no matter what he might unwisely have written. In any case, one hardly expected a woman to run straight to the police with a letter incriminating her lover for the murder of her husband, did one? If, that is, one believed Corinna. Or trusted her, neither of which I did.

Owen seemed to read my mind. "It's gone. The letter, I mean—that's why she was so anxious to see me, to tell me so. She thought he must have found it and meant to use it against her somehow. Against," he amended, "us."

"Gone," I repeated thoughtfully. "How interesting. Did she say she knew for sure he had it? And will she say she was with you this morning?"

If not, matters would begin looking rather ominous, as by not giving Owen an alibi Corinna would be leaving her own whereabouts open to question— unless of course she had some other story for what she'd been doing while Wes got killed, an alibi with just enough room in it for herself.

If, in short, she'd set poor Owen up for Wes's murder.

"I don't know," Owen conceded unhappily. "I haven't been able to reach her, she hasn't gone back to her hotel. Maybe," he added with forlorn hope, "I misunderstood and she meant to go straight to the train. He'd planned to stay overnight, but she might have gone on alone, gone back home. Good God, maybe Corinna doesn't even know he's dead yet."

Right, and maybe I'm the Queen of Sheba. The whole thing was beginning to smell a little rank to me, and to Owen, which was why he was so worried. Wes croaks, Corinna books out of town, and somewhere there's a threatening letter with his name on the signature-line—hey, I'd have been worried, too.

"Let me make sure I've got this straight, Owen. Corinna's husband abused her, she told you about it, and you said—in writing—that you would kill him."

Miserably, Owen agreed with this.

"You knew," I went on, "he would be in town— she'd told you that too, conveniently enough—and where he was going, I suppose? To my office, for some reason?"

As Owen nodded again, another thought struck me. "She didn't tell you why he wanted to see me, by any chance? Or why he didn't call to tell me he was coming?"

It was what the police had asked me, frowning when I said I had no idea. They also asked how Wes knew I would be at the office today, and how, without me, he had managed to get in.

I didn't know that either, and neither did Owen. "We didn't talk about what he was doing here," he said. "We talked about whether or not he had the letter, and if he did what he would do about it. And what *we* should do—which for now was nothing. After all, we couldn't be sure he had it.''

"Right. Terrific. And now you don't know where she is, where the letter is, or whether she'll back up your story about your morning's activities. Not,'' I added, "that it'll do you much good if she does. Once the police get done suspecting you alone, they'll start suspecting you and Corinna together. But if she doesn't back you up you've got more trouble.''

Owen looked aghast.

"Still,'' I told him, "I don't quite see why you've gotten worked up so soon. For all you know, Bell might have simply burned the letter, and unless Corinna's very imprudent''—or very wicked, I thought ''—it could take ages for the police to get around to you. By that time the real murderer might even have been. . . .''

The thump of a heavy iron knocker echoed ominously from downstairs, followed by the patter of Anna's house-slippers and the creak of the big old front door. Next came a heavy tread approaching up the stairs, undeterred by the old housekeeper's quavering protests.

"Oh, no, you can't go up there, Mister Strathmore don't let nobody up there without he strictly invites 'em. You men, now, you come back down here, fix you a nice hot cuppa—oh!''

A solemn knock resounded on the workroom door. "Mr. Strathmore? Police, sir, we'd like a word with you. You mind opening up?''

I signalled Owen frantically. Looking as if he might be about to faint, he dropped the little gun into the ice bowl and closed it into the drinks cabinet. Then, reluctantly, he went to the door and opened it.

In the hall stood two plainclothes policemen, each with badge and ID already displayed. Peering past Owen they spotted me, apparently decided I was harmless, and turned their cool expressionless eyes upon Owen again.

"Sir, we need to ask you about your gun collection."

Gun collection? What gun collection? I stared at Owen.

"The collection," continued the detective, "from which you recently reported several items stolen."

Items? *Stolen*? I smiled sweetly at Owen, imagining his head perched on a spike, whereupon we all trooped downstairs to Owen's gun room, which he also had forgotten to tell me he had.

"Nice collection," I hissed at him, and he cringed.

"Charlotte, I was going to—"

"Oh, can it, Owen. Any thoughts on who might have wanted my manuscripts? Or on who else might have wanted Bell dead? Besides you," I added. "You know, you might have warned me you were armed to the freaking teeth, here."

The guns were in Owen's basement, in a room that unlike the rest of his ramshackle heap had been built in the twentieth century: concrete blocks enamelled a brilliant white, a steel door with a big, expensive-looking lock. Inside, a row of glass cases boasted velvet linings and tasteful indirect light.

The cases held two dozen or more weapons, all meant for showing, not shooting: an 1836 Colt revolving breech pistol, an 1890s French "Apache" six-shooter with a built-in dagger and a knuckle-duster butt, a 1799 Simeon North flintlock pocket-pistol.

And, curiously, one small newer-looking weapon I was quite unable to identify, as unlike the rest it lacked a printed white card bearing its provenance and particulars. Its greasy-grey metal glinted meanly from within the locked glass case; lying there like some mass-produced lump of spite, the ugly little object seemed almost smirkingly aware of its own cheap, unpleasant usefulness.

Owen stared down at it. "Good god," he breathed, "that one isn't mine."

Both policemen turned and looked at him. "Isn't yours?" repeated one of them, not sounding at all as if he believed it.

TWO

LUCKILY, I HAVE refrained from bearing any biological children of my own. I say luckily since if I had, the way I do things I would probably by now have about fourteen of them.

Even without any eggs from my personal basket, however, the number of people who depend on me for decent meals, fresh underwear, clean sheets, and an even minimally adequate supply of affection, instruction, supervision, and companionship tends to turn my kitchen at suppertime into something like a crowd scene out of a Cecil B. DeMille epic.

"Yo," said Myron Rosewater, moonwalking on in with his enormous boom-box to where I was stirring the spaghetti sauce. From the box came a sound as of several young men being poked with, apparently, an electric cattle prod.

Myron was wearing a red and black satin athletic jacket over a black athletic shirt and red sweat pants; on his feet were the kind of expensive white hightops that look as if a pint of air has been pumped into each one.

"Someone took you shopping," I observed. Carefully I made my voice non-judgmental; if half the attempts at rehabilitation that have been applied to Myron were applied to me, I would be Princess Diana by now.

Still, he had stayed in school where by all accounts he was doing nicely, especially in mathematics, economics, and computers—these being the subjects that, at seventeen, Myron thought would prepare him well for his ambition of one day owning half the Western world.

"Doctor Lemon took me," he agreed, bouncing gently from one newly-shod foot to the other. The noise coming out of the boom-box was rap music, which I think is most appropriately named; at least, it always makes me want to rap someone. On the knuckles, preferably with a stout wooden ruler.

"I think," Myron went on, taking in my look and turning the boom-box volume down, "he like to buy me all the clothes he wish he could wear himself."

"Likes to buy what he wishes, you illiterate little peacock, and not unless it's Halloween, thank you." Brushing past Myron, Harry Lemon came in and headed for the pot I was stirring.

"Mmm. A little more garlic, Charlotte, don't you think?" he pronounced. "And perhaps a touch of lemon basil."

Harry was plump, pink and balding, twice the age of Myron whose de facto guardian he had become after getting him out of a street gang and into penny socks. His efforts to improve Myron made him a favorite of the Rosewater family, especially Myron's mother. Myron said when Harry and the Rosewaters got together it looked like the California Raisins entertaining the Pillsbury Doughboy.

When Harry was not buying clothes for Myron or exposing him to higher culture—twi-night double headers alternating with grand opera being the latest examples of this—he was chief medical resident at a local teaching hospital. He was also my friend Helen Terrell's main squeeze, but as Helen had elected to pursue a course of world travel along with her infant son, the offspring of a fellow whose really quite nasty murder I had not long ago cleared her of—

Oh, never mind, it's just too complicated. The up-shot was that Harry was always tired, hungry, and lonesome, and regarded my household as the perfect antidote to this. Tasting the sauce again, he assumed the judicious expression of a rocket scientist wondering if just a bit more thrust might enable him to actually hit the moon.

Personally, I thought any more garlic in this particular batch of spaghetti sauce might enable him to do just that, but since I so enjoy squishing garlic-buds through the little holes in the garlic-bud squisher I tossed in another two or three just to indulge him. As he settled himself with a half-dozen medical journals at the kitchen table, Rob Solli arrived home.

Solli was my main squeeze, or so he liked to think, and as he was merely the most gorgeous creature on earth, and brilliant and affectionate besides, I was inclined to humor him in this regard.

"Mmm," he said, kissing me on the neck while gazing appreciatively over my shoulder at the stove, "spaghetti sauce."

Fortunately my hands were free at the time, as with few exceptions being kissed by Solli has the effect of making me drop whatever I am holding. Among other attractions he has longish blonde hair, blue eyes, and a smile that on the face of a tiger would make jungle explorers draw straws for the privilege of getting eaten up first.

Just now he was wearing a set of decidedly ratty green OR scrub clothes, because like Harry he was also a physician at the medical center. Unlike Harry, however, Solli was a general surgeon, a difference Solli had explained to me by saying that whenever something goes wrong with the human body, the medical guys react by wanting to poke pills into it while surgical guys react by wanting to cut holes into it.

Any minute at least half a dozen people were going to want to put food into it, so I shooed Harry away from the kitchen table and Myron away from the refrigerator and Solli away from me, and called down the hall to where Joey was practicing his transfers—in spite of his limp useless legs he could now go faster from a bed to a wheelchair than I could, and once he got in the chair he could definitely go faster than I could—to remind him to wash his hands before he came out to eat dinner.

"Zoom," he called back, which pretty much summed up his attitude to everything nowadays.

Thinking of this I stood for a moment stunned with sorrow, since in the wake of Joey's spinal surgery the transfers I'd had to practice were mostly mental and after a year I had still not quite gotten the hang of them reliably.

Still, that did not prevent everyone from being hungry so I got out the salad and bread and dumped spaghetti into boiling water, poured glasses of milk for Joey and Myron and Solli along with glasses of wine for Harry Lemon and myself, and set out plates, silverware and napkins for the several additional diners who could be counted upon to come sniffing around the back door just about the time the main course got dished up.

I also set out dishes of grated Romano and Parmesan, one of cottage cheese which I sniffed to make sure it was perfectly fresh, and a small yellow jar of processed cheese food, because Harry Lemon will eat no cheese less than two years old and Joey Rosen abhors any cheese more than two weeks old and Myron Rosewater thinks that cows were placed in their pastures for the specific purpose of providing Cheez Whiz, while Solli and I will eat just about anything providing it sits still long enough for us to plunge our forks into it, and soon after that we all sat happily down to dinner.

Which was when the subject of murder came up again.

"DON'T YOU THINK you're going a little overboard on this?" Solli remarked as he finished loading the plates into Helen's dishwasher, and of course I did not reply that I was already overboard and that what I needed now was a good buoyant life preserver.

A solid clue and a million dollars would come in mighty handy, for example, sometime between now and my *Pen and Pencil* deadline.

Solli did not need to hear such a thing, however, as his reaction whenever I mention money is to point out that he earns enough for all three of us, and why do I have to be so stiff-necked on the topic, anyway?

I glanced around, satisfied that we had returned Helen's kitchen to its usual pristine state: butcher-block oiled and wiped, brushed aluminum polished to a muted sheen, the copper bottoms of the pans glowing rosily from the exposed brick walls.

"No," I replied, reflecting that Helen's place had utterly transformed my housekeeping habits. Key to guilt-free survival in it, I had found, was never leaving anything to soak.

"You should have seen Owen when they took him downtown," I told Solli. "I thought he was going to shiver himself to death. And poor old Anna already had the oven lit, probably getting ready to bake him a cake with a file in it."

"Good," said Solli, unmoved. "He's such an authority on everything, let him do a little honest research for a change."

I already knew he was no fan of Owen Strathmore's, primarily because Owen earned huge sums by cranking out what Solli regarded as toilet tissue with printing on it, while I staggered hopefully along on income derived from the literary equivalent of billboard painting, confining my artistic efforts to what I laughingly called my spare time.

But this was another subject I thought we would be a lot better off ignoring, as it led directly to why I would not let Solli lend me eighteen months' living money so that I could go ahead and write the novel I had been promising to finish for almost a year now. I did not know which scared me more, the idea of owing money to Solli or the idea of actually having to confront the damned novel on a daily basis.

We had covered the mousetraps, the manuscripts, and the body during our usual lively dinnertime conversation, the body of course being an especial point of interest with the boys. Myron wanted to know just how big a hole it was in the guy's forehead, anyway, and Joey wondered what a dead man's fingers really felt like and if by any chance they had clutched at me in ghastly fashion—I got the sense that if they had, it would have made his evening. Harry and Solli commented on topics like degree of lividity, duration of rigor mortis, the clinical aspects of gunshot wounds versus stabbing, cutting, or your ever-popular blunt force injuries, and on an interesting phenomenon called cadaveric spasm that I might have enjoyed hearing more about had I not been trying to enjoy my spaghetti and meat sauce, for heaven's sake.

Meanwhile we had also fed two medical students, a down-on-his-luck aspiring poet whom I was considering offering a job in the offices of *Pen and Pencil*, and a pair of silent and wide-eyed young soul-brothers of Myron's whom I thought had gotten a most unfair impression of what went on at the dinner-table of these strange white people. As Myron mischievously did not offer to enlighten them I supposed I would have to call both their mothers sometime soon.

Not, however, tonight, since while Owen Strathmore was being readied for hauling to the hoosegow he had managed to tell me the time and address of Wesley Bell's writing workshop, held once a month—tonight—in a commons room at one of the Yale colleges.

Owen apparently felt that if I were going to go looking for bloody murderers, I might just as well start in the groves of academe where the vines of spite and envy twined thickest. So tonight I meant to go there and impersonate an unpublished but earnestly aspiring writer, a creature I remembered very well being and which if I thought I would ever have to be again I would just go out and slit my wrists.

Luckily my own published works, while numerous, were not of the type very likely to attract much student scrutiny. Aside from the one novel I had managed to complete—a fictionalized version of my adventures while clearing Helen Terrell of a murder she didn't do—there was my home-help series, including the deathless *A Heck of a Deck* and the even more thrilling *Fun With Formica!*, along with the truly boring but I must say heartwarmingly lucrative *Love That Linoleum!*

Also, there was my two-volume health set, *Tricks for the Sick!* and its sequel *Son of Sick*, the only titles of mine that I have ever really liked. Too bad the publisher who bought them elected instead to call them *What Every Ambulance-Chasing Lawyer Knows*, under the weight of which they dropped as if shot.

Rumor had it those books had their covers ripped off and their contents pulped as they slid from the printing presses, simply to save the cost of sealing them in cartons, and I believed this since I had never seen either of them displayed for sale.

That I had also not seen any advertisements for them was neither here nor there, since my publishers believe that if readers do not already know of a book there is really not much use in trying to convince them it exists, so the money in the ad budget might as well go toward essentials such as another round of vodka gimlets.

"I hope," said Solli, "you are not going to do any following of anyone. Also no clandestine meeting of anyone in alleys, vacant lots, or abandoned buildings."

"Of course not," I assured him, putting on my coat and picking up my pocketbook. I was carrying a dog-eared spiral notebook, as aspiring writers are always equipped with one of these, along with a thickish purple felt-tipped marking pen I thought would banish any lingering aura of professionalism.

"There," I said, "don't I look literary?"

"Eminently," Solli agreed. Then he kissed me, a process which when done by Solli deprives me of all ambition except that of being kissed.

"That," he said, "is just to remind you to come back."

"Oh, I will," I promised, already looking hopefully ahead to this event. Then with considerable regret I left my little love-nest, so brightly and cozily furnished with its warmly glowing lamps and my warmly glowing boyfriend, to go out and infiltrate a nest of vipers.

I SUPPOSE THAT somewhere in the English-speaking world there is someone who does not want to be a writer, has never wanted to be a writer, and who if he or she by accident ever did become a writer would promptly stop being one in favor of some more normal activity such as sword-swallowing or camel-racing. Wherever he or she may have been that evening, however, I can report with certainty that it was not at Wesley Bell's workshop.

"Oh," said the gaunt young woman in the long black dress, eyeing me doubtfully from the doorway of the Peters-Darrow commons room on the campus of Yale University. For a moment I thought she must be in mourning for Wes Bell, but then I realized: she was a serious poet, and thus required always to resemble a finalist in the Morticia Adams look-alike contest.

"If you've come to try to join the workshop," she said, sizing me up dismissively, "you're too late. Wes Bell's dead."

I fluttered with inarticulate surprise while she went on eyeing my flat shoes, denim skirt, little white blouse, and shapeless coat, all put on to give precisely the impression she was now absorbing from them: that of a woman who longed to express herself and get published and show everyone, especially her husband, that she really was too a sensitive person with deeper thoughts than he could possibly fathom, but when he finally understood her needs it would be too late, she would divorce him anyway and run away with a man who wore tweed jackets and smoked a pipe.

Pityingly, the serious poet waved me in to rub elbows with the workshop members, one of whom really did have on a tweed jacket and was smoking a pipe, although I was not in the slightest tempted to run away with him as there is something about a walrus moustache and green teeth that always puts me off any romantic notions I may be harboring.

"Sherry?" He leered at me, proffering a glass. It smelled like the stuff you use to strip varnish off old woodwork, but I accepted it anyway and smiled back.

"I'm terribly sorry about your friend," I said, gesturing ineffectively. "Colleague, I mean. Whatever you real writers call it."

Hopeless, helpless, harmless; standing there in that genteel little chamber with its leaded-glass casements, faded tapestries and fusty unread classics, breathing in an atmosphere of sweat and book-dust, I fairly radiated awe and the simple desire to be edified. Already half-drunk, Mister Walrus Moustache took it down in one unsuspecting gulp.

"I called him an ass," he said cheerfully, "and I call him one now. A dead ass, and us well rid of him." As he spoke he sloshed out another glass of the despicable sherry.

"Goodness," I said. "Do you mean he was a . . . scoundrel?"

"Hah!" His amusement gusted on a cloud of booze and nicotine. "You have, my dear, a gift for the consummate phrase. I'm assuming of course you are a writer? Or perhaps," he added suggestively, "in the long and arduous process of becoming one?"

I half-expected him to twirl the dripping moustache. "I scribble," I admitted with a show of reluctance, and simpered prettily again, there being only so much fluttering I could do without actually rising up off the floor.

"Nothing as good as your work, I'm sure," I added, and he smirked in satisfied acknowledgment of this. "But what did he do—Mr. Bell, I mean—to make you call him that? I always thought he was so...well, so eminent."

"Hmph," the Walrus said. "For one thing, he had the effrontery to claim *Harlan's Heart* was his idea when everyone here knows he stole it from David Fischer. By the mantel, the one with the tragic-hero look, you can't miss him."

I followed his inebriated nod in the direction of a tall, slender fellow with mussed black hair, deep brooding eyes, and a pouting mouth whose shape suggested gross sensuality combined with the bitter taste of complete career dissatisfaction.

Just now the object of my scrutiny appeared unable to decide whether he was impersonating Mick Jagger or Algernon Swinburne, a problem I thought might crimp almost any career but especially a literary one; a man unable to characterize himself can hardly be expected reliably to characterize other people, it seems to me.

"What sort of thing did you say you write?" breathed the Walrus, following this with the suggestion that whatever sort of thing it was, we really ought to get together privately—say, possibly tomorrow afternoon at three, his place—so he could give me the benefit of his expertise on it.

When I got over being astonished, I thought that anyone who would put such a crude set of moves on the sort of vulnerably innocent character I was impersonating really ought to keep his nose-hairs better trimmed, preferably with a pair of electric hedge-clippers.

"Obituaries," I informed him sweetly, slipping out of his groping range and heading for the young man by the mantelpiece.

"Hello," I tried, approaching him. "I wonder, could you possibly explain something to me?"

He glowered down through the smoke from his Gauloise Bleu. "Don't know. Depends on how bright you are, doesn't it?"

"Perhaps," I allowed, wondering how such a rude young man had managed to live so long. This one had entered first grade, I calculated, on or about the date of my first marriage.

"The thing is, though," I pressed him, "I thought this was supposed to be a writing workshop."

The young man let out a harsh despairing laugh.

"But no one's doing anything except drinking and talking," I complained, "except you. I mean aren't we all supposed to read aloud from our works in progress, or something?"

The young man straightened, peering curiously at me. "And what am I doing?" he asked, smiling lazily as he seized upon his favorite topic.

"Thinking?" I ventured. He wore a black turtle-neck sweater, denim jacket and narrow jeans, a wide leather belt whose brass buckle looked as if it might make a pretty fair bludgeoning tool, and leather boots.

"Thinking," he agreed darkly. "But if I told you what I was thinking about you'd probably run screaming from the room."

The idea made him look hopeful. "Anyway," he
went on, "if a workshop is what you've come for,
you've come on the wrong night. All that's going to go
on here this evening is a lot of dirt-dishing and Bell-
bashing."

How convenient, I thought. "That man over there
says he stole your book." I pointed. "That Mr. Bell
did, I mean. Is it true?" I tried to look wide-eyed.

"He told you that, did he?" The young man smiled
sadly. "Stupid old Reginald, I hope you didn't let him
get his paws on you. But he's right about the book.
Harlan's Heart was all my idea, I'd slaved on the thing
for years. Characters, settings—I could have written
that book in my sleep."

Why didn't you? I thought, but as this cut rather
near my own bones I didn't say it. "And then what
happened?"

"Then," he said bitterly, "I told him. I mean, I was
an undergraduate, never published, and he was a pro-
fessor, a *creative writing* teacher—" his lips twisted
poisonously on the words—"who'd had stories in the
North American Review. I thought he was some kind
of paragon. Someone to look up to, give me a few
pointers, for Christ's sake. God, I was naive."

His laugh was mirthless. "And let that be a lesson
to you, little Mrs. Wanna-Be or whatever your name
is. If you're a real writer you only need two pointers—one to point your butt at the writing-chair and
the other one to point your fingers at the typewriter.
The rest," he finished, "is complete bullshit, especially this." He gestured at the room, hopelessly.

He was so damned right I could only stand there and stare, and after a moment I think it must have made him nervous.

"But that's not what you want to know," he snarled, "is it? You want some juicy gossip you can take back to the suburbs, impress all your mommy-hubby friends while you sit around the gas grill."

He lit another cigarette, spewed a thin stream of smoke. "What the hell, I'll oblige, entertain the masses. I went out drinking with the guy one night during break, what a thrill, man, sitting at a booth in Mory's knocking 'em back with Wesley Bell. I felt just like Norman Mailer, you know? And when he asked me what I was working on, I told him."

"All of it?" I asked, and he gave me that percep-tive look again.

"All of it," he said flatly. "Last rounds, I'm still blabbing out the story, he's sitting there looking at me like I just flew in from Mars. Only I didn't notice that, how intent he was. Not until later. I figured he was just interested."

"And?" I prompted him.

He stared at his burning cigarette. "And then he says to me, very softly and seriously like he's making some pronouncement from on high, 'Mr. Fischer,' he says, 'my advice to you is go home and learn a trade. You're wasting your time, you'll never be a real writer. Why not try something you *can* do?'"

I felt my jaw drop. "That's the cruelest thing I've ever heard."

The young man laughed a little. "Oh, I don't know. Maybe it was the smartest. The next day classes were scheduled to start back up, but Bell didn't meet any of his classes. He never taught another English class again, and a little over a year after I told him the story, *Harlan's Heart* came out. I guess even you must know what happened after that."

I knew. And if the tale I'd just heard was even halfway true, I had to give this fellow credit: he might look a little sullen but he wasn't gnashing his teeth or tearing his hair out by the fistful.

Which was what I would have been doing in his place, since the storm of praise and glory that greeted *Harlan's Heart* didn't end when Bell walked off with the Trout prize. The book brought a million-dollar advance and was snapped up at once for a movie that stormed the nation's theaters, while also being scripted for a radio drama, produced as a television series, and in one particularly unlikely adaptation transformed into a ballet.

"But," I protested, "how did he get away with it? Couldn't you do something? Tell people, sue him, something?"

He shrugged. "Nope. That was the worst part. See, that night when Wes Bell told me I was hopeless, that I'd never be a writer—well, I believed him." He laughed softly.

"So," he went on, "I went home and burnt it. Every bit of it, every notebook, even the old envelopes I'd made notes on the backs of. When I was done, not a word was left. Not," he finished sadly, "a single word."

Of proof, he meant; anybody can claim he wrote a book, or that he confided in someone the completely plotted, thoroughly fleshed-out idea for one. Coming up with the evidence, though, is something else again.

"Well," I said inadequately, "you can write another novel, can't you? Just come up with another good idea, and—"

But of course it was not nearly as simple as that. "Sure," the young man said, he smiled undeceived, "another one. Only somehow I just haven't quite felt up to it. Haven't quite got the stomach for it, you know."

His glowering look returned. "Anyway, that's my little tale of woe. Feel free to entertain with it at your next card party, or whatever nice ladies like you do for fun. And if you ever do really write anything—"

He peered down at me. "You might, you know, something about you makes me think you might. So if you do, and someone tries telling you the writing business is anything but a bloody shark pool, you remember: either they don't know their ass from page eight or they're trying to get the first bite."

As he spoke, the serious poet drifted over possessively.

"Playing Ancient Mariner again, are we, David? Taking the great man's name in vain for the umpteenth time? Better watch out—someone might get the idea you blew Bell's head off."

Not entirely off, exactly, I wanted to say, but of course I didn't. The serious poet seemed in her funereal way to be on the make for David Fischer, looping her arm through his and leaning tipsily against him, to which he looked resigned.

"Well," I said, "it was nice talking with you. And I wish you luck on your new book."

"New book?" she asked suspiciously, and I understood; one's own production however lightweight always does look so much more substantial beside another writer's outright block, and Fischer was blocked monumentally. Beside him, the serious poet no doubt felt prolific.

Thinking this, I eased my way back to the drinks table where the awful sherry had been replaced by an enormous bottle of Gallo Red. Pleased, I poured myself a glassful and looked around for another target. At least a dozen more people had crowded in, some of them already quite drunk, and the level of sound in the room had risen to a dull roar.

I was sipping my wine, wondering if the usefulness of this gathering had passed—half the people around me weren't talking about Bell, now, and some did not seem even to have known him—when someone bumped me from behind, swore, and turned furiously.

It was Corinna Bell.

"What the hell are you doing here," Corinna asked with her usual surplus of charm, "and where did you get that awful stuff you're wearing?"

I'd met Corinna through my friend Helen Terrell, back when they both had attended a private finishing school for young ladies. There they had absorbed the proper method of pouring tea, what to say when meeting royalty, and how to walk with dictionaries—real or imagined—balanced on the tops of their heads, all skills remaining shaky in my own deportment, but ones I have made up for by knowing how to lick peanut butter off a sharp knife.

On this evening of deep connubial mourning, Corinna wore a little black number with a plunging vee neckline, three-quarter-length fitted sleeves, and a short sheath skirt. It made her look slim and fatal as a hidden switchblade, and I thought she'd probably had her French dressmaker run it up for her the minute she found out her husband was dead.

The question in my mind concerned just which minute that was.

"Nice running into you again, too," I told her, restraining myself from seizing those sweet fragile collarbones and shaking her until her eyes rolled back.

"Talked with Owen Strathmore lately, have you?" I added maliciously. "He said he was having some trouble getting in touch. Wanted to send along his condolences, I suppose."

Her eyes contracted into little slits. "Owen," she spat, "that lying bastard. Because of him, I spent the day with police officers."

The way she said it, they might have been diphtheria germs. "In a horrid little office," she went on, "with a lot of sweaty little civil servants in cheap suits. Can you believe they offered me *instant* coffee? In a *styrofoam* cup, if you can imagine that. And when I refused, they just kept gobbling up their greasy sandwiches, making pigs of themselves right there in front of me." She shuddered at the distastefulness of it.

"Corinna," I said gently, "about Owen, though—"

She didn't seem too broken up over Wesley, but then maybe she was just being brave.

"Owen's lying about me," she snapped, "they're all lying, now that Wes is dead and can't stop them. I only came here to find out what sort of things they'd be saying about him."

A glimmer of practiced spite came into her face. "Most of them don't know me. How would they? Poor little schoolteachers with inky fingers and bad haircuts and no social standing at all. So I've been letting them make their vicious remarks to my face, and then I've been telling them who I am."

She pronounced the last three words each with a slight separate emphasis, three little stabs that made me think of a cruel child plunging pins into a bug. She was lovely to look at; delightful, perhaps, to hold. And equipped, in addition, with all the spiritual depth and emotional sensitivity of a department-store mannequin.

I wondered what in the world Owen thought he had been doing with her. "So you weren't with Owen this morning," I pressed. "You didn't meet him at a different hotel, and stay with him until eleven-thirty?"

Corinna's lip curled daintily. "Don't be absurd. Of course I wasn't. I've never been alone with the man in my life. Thank god," she added.

"And you aren't missing any letter from Owen, saying he was going to get rid of your husband, who had been abusing you?"

"Good heavens, Charlotte, what is this? Don't those little things you try to write keep you busy enough? Your little guides for the terminally inept, or whatever they are?''

She was eyeing me amusedly now and I got that pin-in-the-bug feeling again, only this time the thorax was my own.

"And—" I hesitated, then decided the hell with it— "Wes didn't steal the idea for *Harlan's Heart*? Specifically from that guy over there by the mantelpiece?''

"David Fischer," she replied without having to look, "was an amusement of mine until he became too insistent. He wanted me to go off with him—to live in a garret, I suppose, and eat things out of cans." Her dismissive laugh was silvery.

"He hasn't the imagination for *Harlan's Heart*, or for much of anything else once the thrill wears off— and believe me, my dear, I'm the one who ought to know. Poor David," she finished, not sounding sad, "I'm afraid he's just a novelty item."

Then she peered at me. "Really, though—why all this interest? I mean, just because whoever did it happened to catch up with Wesley in your office—"

"Catch up?" It was a curious turn of phrase. "Had someone been following him?"

For the first time, Corinna looked uncomfortable. "There was something bothering him," she admitted, "I know that much. Some phone calls he didn't like, and I think some letters, ones he disappeared with into his den. He wouldn't come out for hours."

The trouble with Corinna, I'd learned long ago, was that when she lied she also believed the lie herself. Inside her tiny body was an ego so huge, she really believed she could rearrange the past simply by saying it so.

Still . . . "When was that?"

She shrugged. "About a month ago. I think Owen must have wanted something out of Wesley and whatever it was Wesley wouldn't give it to him, so Owen killed him. And now he's made up a story about being with me for an alibi, although why in the world he thought I'd go along with it I can't imagine. Owen is such a child."

Frowning, she practically stamped her little foot. "Why do people have to be so awful, anyway?" she demanded.

I thought it surely would have been nicer for Corinna if the rest of the world cleared the way when it saw her coming, so she could go about her intensely self-absorbed business without all that irritating riff-raff constantly cluttering up the place.

Nicer for the rest of the world, too, lots of times, as poor David Fischer had apparently discovered.

"So, you told the police all that?" I asked her.

It was getting to be time to go; my glass was nearly empty, and I did not want to have another drink, as if I did I would have to ask Solli to come pick me up—either that or ask Corinna for a ride home, than which I would rather choke on my own spit. Solli was a good man, a fine companion and faithful as the day is long, but in her salad days I'd seen Corinna take men very much like him and turn them into a substance resembling naval jelly, and that was before she'd even had much practice.

She tossed her head defiantly. "Of course I did. I told them I was in the hotel room, my *own*, all morning with a headache, and that if they had any more intrusive questions they could just call up my lawyer and then we'd see who wound up being put on the defensive like some common criminal. Gritty little men in K-Mart shoes and awful ties. All policemen must be color-blind, or something."

I managed to suppress a smile. "And did they believe you? About your being alone in your room, that is."

At this her face smoothed happily, whether with the novel pleasure of simple honesty or the fun of putting one over on me I could not tell.

"Of course they believed me, Charlotte, naturally they did." Tipping her glass back, she drained it and set it with a decisive little click down on the table.

"I mean," she finished with a transparent smile, "why would I lie?"

THREE

By TUESDAY AFTERNOON the office was cleaned up, the carpet gotten rid of and the blotter replaced, and things were back to normal which is to say that I was broke, desperate, and without an idea in the world of what to do next.

I had to have an issue of the magazine, so I could get paid. I couldn't take money from Solli; before him, my record in the romance department was Cupid fourteen, me nothing, and I really did not want to mess up this one. The thing is, you start taking money from someone and the next thing you know you are feeling chronically beholden to that someone, and right after that you start punishing them for it, which last time I looked was not on *Cosmo's* list of the "Ten Fool-Proof Ways of Keeping Him Warm For Your Form."

So: action. I'd hired the down-and-out poet and set him to listing some article ideas, and he was now at his desk cranking out the first of them. "The Hot-Shot Plot" described a method for cobbling up a story-line out of good guys, bad guys, and a useful little item called a fatal flaw, which I imagined as a crack in a character's soul sort of like the one in the Liberty Bell: you smack it hard enough, *something* interesting is bound to happen.

Over in the corner one of the typists was answering letters from subscribers; I figured in a pinch we could run these as a special column called The Teacher Feature, and fill up a few more pages with them. Right now the typist was replying to a fellow who liked to write storys (his spelling) but had heard that writing articuls payed better, so would we please tell him what the diffrense was.

At the bottom of this, block-printed in a whimsical mix of lower-case and capitals, was a PS requesting that we let him know Right Away as he was getting quite short of money.

This set me to planning yet another *Pen and Pencil* piece, on how to make a small fortune by writing—the first step of course being to start with a large fortune. I was trying to think of a snappy lead to start it off with when the mailman came in, bearing a small package wrapped in brown grocery-bag paper.

"Charlotte Kent?" he inquired. I said yes, that was me, so he tossed the package on the desk and went out.

"Did we order something?" I asked, getting up to see what it was, but I didn't think we had and the package was too small to be an unsolicited manuscript. How come the mailman never brings me any of those when I need them, I thought irritably, tugging on the string—which was when the package blew up.

I put my hands to my face: red. Dripping from my nose, my eyebrows, and my chin...wonderful, I thought, beginning to feel a little faint, I have just been transformed into next year's facial reconstructive-surgery poster girl.

I waited for the pain to arrive, to lend even further vivid interest to my dying moments. But none did and to my surprise the moments didn't, either, because the red stuff dripping off me was ink.

"Wow," said the typist, staring over from her typewriter, on which she had been explaining that yes, a play about the relationship between an autistic boy and a 1929 Model T certainly did sound interesting, but unfortunately we did not publish true-life experiences, however well-dramatized.

"Gosh," said the poet, blinking up from where he had been explaining that having everybody get run over by a truck on the final page was not an effective ending for a story unless it was an "experimental" story, in which case one would do well to make the ending as inconclusive as one could, and if possible also as incomprehensible—by putting it at the beginning, for instance.

"Don't," I said sourly, "everyone rush to help at once."

Red ink, a now-shredded plastic bagful of it, triggered by a powerful spring attached to the string I had been tugging on. Once I had washed the stuff off my hands and face—to my surprise it came off easily and without leaving any stain—I gingerly examined the remains of the package.

Inside, wrapped in waxed paper, was a note. SEE HOW EASY IT IS WHY NOT MIND YOUR OWN BUSINESS I CAN GET AT YOU ANY TIME.

"Well," gulped the typist, beginning to look a little green, "that's sure not a very funny joke. None of this is, in fact."

Then she opened a file drawer and took out her purse and faced me. "You know, Miss Kent, I didn't think I'd mind working up here, I mean after the...the incident and all, and I'm really sorry to leave you in the lurch this way, but now I'm starting to feel kind of funny and I think—"

"That's all right," I said, "I understand. I'll mail you your last week's pay, all right?"

Gratefully she agreed and pattered off down the stairs, for which I could not blame her; I was feeling kind of funny, too.

"How about you?" I asked the down-on-his-luck poet, whom I did not really expect to be worried about a little red ink since for one thing his checkbook was already swimming in it. I felt sure his landlady regularly sent him notes a lot more threatening than the one I had just received.

"You know," he said, "I am a totally non-violent person."

Then he recited a lot of stuff about staying centered and keeping his energies focused and protecting his karma from contamination, all of which meant he was getting the hell out of Dodge just as swiftly as possible, because there is only one thing worse than being a down-on-your-luck poet and that is being a dead down-on-your-luck poet, especially if it happens before you have managed to get a single poem published.

The poet pattered gratefully on down the stairs, leaving me with two unfinished articles, four unthought-of articles, twenty-five unanswered items of reader mail plus one threatening note and an exploded letter-bomb.

And that would have been the end of the poet-and-typist story except that as I found out later they met accidentally at the coffee shop on the corner where they'd gone to drown their sorrows—she in a tuna-fish sandwich and a diet soda, he in a jelly doughnut, a milkshake, and a chocolate brownie.

And youth being what it is, and both of them being classic movie addicts, they convinced themselves that all of this was just like an Alfred Hitchcock film and they were just like the young Jimmy Stewart and the young Katharine Hepburn in it—only not, of course, if they ran out on their parts.

Which I supposed left me for the part of Yap the Wonder Dog. Still, I was very glad to see them when they came trooping back together holding hands, both of them all smiling and shiny-faced.

So I set them once more to their appointed tasks, which they attacked with renewed enthusiasm now that they saw my office as a sort of stage set with themselves in a pair of pink spotlights at the center of it. The fact that it now felt to me like ground zero no longer appeared to worry them.

The poet finished the whole first draft of "Hot-Shot Plot" and brought it to me for my editorial approval. I smiled gently at him and told him it was fine, just fine. It scanned and parsed beautifully while making absolutely no real-life sense whatsoever, a prime characteristic of almost all *Pen and Pencil* material. Next he was planning a piece about how to get ideas, which I always think is like teaching someone to have freckles but he was all enthused about it so I nodded and told him to knock himself out.

Across from him the typist had worked her way through five more letters, and was now on one that complained in injured tones about how mean all magazine editors were, as after the author had put in all that work on her story about a girl who liked to burn down peoples' houses you would think they could at least tell her why they would not buy it, including their home addresses in case she needed to get in touch with them on matters of Crucial Importance, and by the way what was Miss Kent's home address?

I asked the typist to return this letter with Miss Kent's name marked 'Deceased'. Considering recent events that came close enough to the truth to fight its way past my conscience.

Finally I returned to my own thoughts, which focused on the question of who knew I was taking an interest in Wesley Bell's murder.

There was Owen Strathmore, of course. His tale about having spent the morning with Corinna Bell was so far unsupported and the strange gun from his collection-room had not yet completed ballistics testing. Still, his cockamamie theory about a burglar coming back to plant the gun on him was so wild, I thought I was probably his only hope, and as he thought so too I doubted he had sent me any exploding ink-packages.

Then there was Corinna Bell herself, so talented at figuring out what other people wanted and making sure they didn't get it. She seemed to feel there was only so much pleasure in the world, and that the more

she could ruin for someone else the more of it would
be left for herself.

Fifteen years ago, visiting Helen at school, I had
rescued a fallen butterfly chrysalis Corinna had been
about to stomp upon, delivering it instead to another
girl whom I knew collected them.

True to her nature Corinna had not forgotten it, and
if she were not the widow of the murdered man I might
have suspected her of sending the ink-bomb. She was
perfectly capable of doing such a thing, just to put a
wrench in my monkey-works. But the other thing she
never forgot was the location of her own best inter-
ests; even to her, a cruel prank was not worth being
implicated in a murder.

She might, of course, have told someone else who I
really was:

The walrus-moustached Lothario, who bore no love
for Wesley Bell and felt the rest of the world had been
done a favor, too.

Or perhaps David Fischer, whose life Bell had ruined by stealing his book and spoiling his creative appetite.

Or any of the rest in attendance at Bell's strange
wake-without-a-corpse: jealous colleagues, rejected
collaborators, resentful ex-lovers, even possibly an
obsessed fan or two. The list of people who might have
murdered Bell, I thought, was long and colorful.

Almost as colorful as the ink someone had splashed
in my face. And that, I thought, was a mistake.

"Listen, you two," I told the typist and the poet,
"take that stuff you're doing home. Just keep track of

your hours and get it all done, and bring it to my house tomorrow morning.''

"But Miss Kent," said the typist, "I've nearly finished answering this letter from a fellow who wants to know why he shouldn't write his essays in purple ink on yellow construction paper, so they'll stand out from all the worthless junk the editor of *The Atlantic Monthly* has been buying on account of not having *his* thoughts on life to publish."

"But Miss Kent," said the poet, "I'm almost finished with the part where I explain that to get really good ideas you have to sit on a hard wooden chair in front of a computer screen or a typewriter or god forbid a spiral notebook for ten years, writing reams and reams of complete and utter crap just to get it out of your system, while everyone else you've ever heard of is watching television or going out on dates and having kids and being promoted to company vice-president. Meanwhile your friends are laughing at you and your enemies are triumphing over you and—"

"That's all right," I interrupted him gently, "I'm sure you can describe the normal apprenticeship of the aspiring writer just as well at home in your own little hovel as you can here."

At that he laughed, which was when I begin to think he might actually write a decent poem someday, and he must have thought so too because he packed up all his stuff and went bravely out the office door, whistling.

I smiled at the typist and she smiled at me as his footsteps clattered in a carefree manner down the stairs; a moment later we heard the door to the street creak open, followed by a thump like the sound of a very ripe cantaloupe breaking, and although I cannot be sure I think it was then that I understood what trouble we had gotten into, the poet of course most of all.

"Oh dear god," the typist said, and from her tone I knew she understood it, too; by the time I got downstairs she had already reached him, crouched by him briefly, and sprinted for the phone booth across the street. As I knelt by his body I saw her pushing buttons in the sort of clear-headed determined way that I have never been able to achieve in emergencies.

"Don't feel bad." The down-and-out poet smiled weakly. "I didn't want to tell anyone, but I have a sonnet coming out next month in *Poetry* magazine."

"That's wonderful. You must be looking forward to that." I bit my cheeks, trying not to let him see me cry.

"Yes." His lovely foolish face was covered in blood. "It means—it means I'm a success. It means—" he winced—"it was all worth it." He closed his eyes.

"Of course you are," I murmured to him. "Of course it was."

Beside him lay the concrete block somebody had engineered up onto the doorframe in some horridly cunning manner, its jagged corner all smutched with the poet's blood.

"Now you just lie still, all right? Everything's okay, you are going to be just fine. In a minute the ambulance will come to take you to the—"

Then I realized that the down-and-out poet did not need me to tell him to lie still. Lying still had just become his specialty.

And finding whoever did this to him had just become mine.

"EVERYONE," I told Owen Strathmore, "and I mean everyone who might have had a reason to want to kill Wesley Bell."

"Charlotte," Owen replied exhaustedly, "I might as well hand you the Manhattan telephone directory. Just passing him on the street was enough to make most people want to see him staked out on an anthill."

It was half-past seven. I had cooked dinner and fed the starving hordes, done the dishes and checked up on Joey's English homework, all the while harboring a trembling fury so great even Myron Rosewater kept quiet, helpfully clearing the table and rinsing plates and never once going near the boom-box.

Owen had been assigned a quarter-million dollar bail and released temporarily, after his lawyer explained to the court that almost all of Owen's considerable fortune was tied up in antique literature, a commodity that was notoriously hard to dispose of on short notice and one Owen would no more abandon—even to escape a murder charge—than he would chop off his own typing-fingers.

Now he sat at the table in Anna's spotless kitchen, peering through those fingers at the wreckage that had been his life.

"Okay," I said as Anna dithered in the pantry, searching out further supplies of little treats and sweetmeats; at intervals she appeared with doilied plates of these, as apparently she felt that candied pistachios would help Owen keep his strength up.

"Okay, let's go back a little. They say the gun they found downstairs is the murder weapon, and you say you've never seen it before and don't know how it got there."

"Correct," said Owen, biting morosely into a petit-four and washing it down with Jack Daniels.

"Furthermore you say you spent all morning with Corinna, but she says you didn't, and not only that she says she's never been involved with you at all and never got any letter from you. A letter you say showed your motive to murder Bell, one she told you—*you* say she told you—she did get and was missing."

"Right again." He picked up a little sandwich with the crusts cut off, examined it without enthusiasm, and bit into it.

"A letter," I said, waiting for him to catch on, "that your lawyers say is now in the hands of the police."

"Yes, but—oh." Owen blinked in puzzlement. "That's how they knew to come to me. But how did they get hold of it so fast? I thought—"

"Exactly. You thought there would be an investigation, that the murdered man's wife would naturally come under suspicion, and that in the course of things her involvement with you would be revealed and then you would be suspected. Meanwhile the letter would turn up, perhaps among Bell's papers, and bingo, the trap closes. But it didn't happen that way, did it?"

"No." He frowned, chewing. "It was as if they had it at once, maybe before Bell even—"

I smiled at him through my own clenched teeth. "Precisely. Before he died, or very soon afterwards. Which strikes me as just a wee bit too convenient, doesn't it seem so to you? In fact, it strikes me as a plan."

"But—not Corinna. Not that sweet, harmless little..."

"Owen," I told him impatiently, "wise up. She's about as harmless as a cross between a pit-bull and a black-widow spider. As a matter of fact, you're probably lucky all this happened. If you'd kept on with her, when she got done with you there'd be nothing left but a little pile of bones and hair."

His mouth dropped downwards. "I suppose you're right. If she loved me she'd be telling the truth about me now. I guess," he finished sadly, "I'm not much like the fellows I write about."

"No," I told him, "you're not, thank god. The world has enough violent, macho maniacs running around in it without your bulk swelling up the ranks."

He glanced shamefacedly at his plate, which he had cleaned without realizing it. Instantly Anna placed another one in front of him, this one loaded with cheese and cold cuts.

"Can't I fix a little bite of something for you too, Miss?" she inquired in tones of concern. "You look sort of peaky-like, you don't mind my sayin' so. I know," she brightened, "I've got just the thing," and before I could protest she scuffled away to the pantry again.

As she went, she bestowed a look of such ferocious loyalty and love upon Owen that I thought he might just as well fire his lawyer and let Anna defend him; she had not forgiven herself for allowing the policemen upstairs and in the wake of this lapse was uninclined to let him out of her sight, lest someone do him some injury she could not avenge on the spot.

"The thing is, Owen," I said when she was out of earshot—for although she denied it Anna was rather deaf—"someone gave the police that letter. Your lawyers say they have it, and that means—"

"That means," he thumped his big fist triumphantly down onto Anna's blue-checked oilcloth, "I wrote it in the first place. It shows I'm telling the truth about it, that the letter did in fact exist."

Then his face fell again. "And that puts me back in the soup, doesn't it? I wrote a threatening letter about Bell and now he's dead."

"But Owen, why did you write it? That's the thing, don't you see? Because either you're an utterly deluded self-deceiving fool—which I wouldn't for a moment deny under other circumstances, but this is murder we're talking about—or you had a reason to write it. The reason being that you were romantically involved with Corinna, and she told you her husband was abusive to her. And this of course made you very angry."

As, I thought, it might have been intended to. Still, other people could have known about the letter and decided it would come in handy, as part of a recipe for creating the soup Owen was now stewing in.

By lying about her relationship with Owen, Corinna might only be trying to save some shred of her already checkered reputation—which left the field wide open as far as I was concerned for someone else, although I was not yet letting Corinna off the hook, either, since when live ones are made into dead ones I feel who could possibly have better motive than their nearest and dearest, and murder statistics bear me out in this.

Bell himself was shaping up into a slime toad, the sort of fellow who has two separate and distinct personalities: one for public consumption, the other for getting his sadistic rocks off.

Which brought me back to the hate-list. Just then, however, Anna pattered back, bearing a suspicious-looking steaming beaker.

"Now, Miss, I want you to just drink this down. Don't you worry, it ain't got no liquor in it, nor nothing else neither as could put a damper on them nice bright brain-cells of yours. I just stewed you up a portion of my Aunt Sally's secret recipe herbal tea, the goings-in of which'll put new hairs on a dead man's corpuscles as I do hope sincerely it'll do for yours."

"Charlotte," Owen began doubtfully, "I don't think—"

The stuff tasted like beetles decomposing in pondwater and had a kick like a team of Clydesdales. I took a bigger swallow and felt my spine straighten into a perfect vertical column; if there'd happened to be any forty-story buildings nearby, I'd have gone out and leapt them just for the sheer pleasure of it.

"Now," I said, looking around for some steel to bend in my bare hands, "about those enemies of Bell's."

Owen must have seen something new in my eyes as at my request he sat up too and for the first time began seriously to think. Ten minutes later I had three names. The first belonged to David Fischer, whom of course I already knew. The second was a critic's and when he mentioned it I glanced questioningly at him, as it is more usual for writers to want to murder critics than the other way around.

"She's in *Harlan's Heart*," he explained. "Depends on your point of view whether you think it's caricature or crucifixion, but he put her in there, all right. Most unflattering portrayal, she's been furious about it ever since. Especially," he added, "since there's not a damned thing she can do about it."

"Why not bring suit for libel, collect damages? I mean, if she's really all that recognizable—"

Owen shook his head. "You haven't read the book, I gather. You must be the only person in the world who hasn't. Do, and you'll see why Phileta Poole doesn't want more publicity than she's already had."

"All right. And who's the third one?"

Three, I thought would be plenty to begin with. The first fine rush of the atomic tea was wearing off, and although I still felt as if I could memorize the Oxford English Dictionary merely by placing it under my pillow, I was beginning to suspect there might be more sizzle than steak to this sensation.

"Reginald Symonds," Owen said. "Local fellow, been writing what he calls serious fiction since before the deluge. Same book over and over, really, thin stuff about his childhood which I gather was spent in one tar-paper shack after another. How he got beaten up, groped his first girl, and came to the city. Reginald finds his own adolescence fascinating, which I suppose is why he can't seem to get out of it.''

"Big moustached fellow, kind of moth-eaten?"

"Like the cowardly lion with a case of mange," Owen agreed. "Breath like an animal, too. Read his stuff?''

"No, but I just met him. He didn't strike me as a murderer."

"Wait," Owen advised, "until you see what he does with the English language. I've got one of Reggie's books around here, I think, and a copy of *Harlan*. You can take them both."

"Thanks." I got up, which was when I discovered the other thing about Anna's tea: it didn't just wear off. It also took with it every molecule of whatever the human nervous system uses for insulation.

Suddenly I knew how those Russian women feel, the ones who claim they can see colors through their fingertips. Right then I felt sure I could hear Beethoven's Fifth through my taste-buds. The linoleum rippled, then did a buck-and-wing—or I did one, I wasn't sure—before the roaring in my ears settled down to a gentle, steady hiss.

"Tried to warn you about that stuff," Owen said, lumbering ahead of me down the hallway toward the front door.

"But don't worry, the effects wear off in a day or so."

In the dark hallway the tall old bookshelves bent forward, the books whispering interestedly among themselves and the ivy in the wallpaper writhing at me, sly eager tendrils reaching out and coiling back.

"Except for the psychotic flashbacks, of course," Owen added reassuringly. "Ah, here we are." He pulled down two volumes.

"Don't read Reggie's lying down, it'll put you in a coma," he advised. "The guy wants to make money on his books, he should try reading them aloud to insomniacs."

"And the other one?" *Harlan's Heart* had a dust-jacket patterned in psychedelic hearts: pink, blue, yellow, chartreuse, and purple, all on a sharp black background. Every heart had a thin silver arrow stuck through it, a crimson droplet suspended from the point of each arrow-tip.

Owen frowned down at Bell's book while seeming to weigh it in his hands. "I think," he said slowly, "this book deserved every word of praise it got. That's why Reggie hated Bell so much—not that *Harlan* was bad, but that it was good. Same sort of thing poor Reggie'd been trying for years, but his are all grey mush and every time he does one it's greyer and mushier."

He handed the book to me. "By the way, that's also why I don't believe David Fischer's story. Stealing *Harlan* may be the one despicable thing Wes Bell *didn't* do, during his despicable existence."

"I'm not sure I understand," I said through the waves still pounding in my ears. My lips felt like rubbery slabs of liver. Lucky I don't have gum in my mouth, I thought, or I wouldn't be able to walk. I stifled a giggle as Owen eyed me sternly.

"Charlotte, are you sure you're absorbing all this?"

Serious again, I nodded. "I'm listening, Owen. But if Wes was such a rat, why couldn't he have based his best-seller on the story David Fischer told him? After he had destroyed Fischer's confidence, he could be pretty sure Fischer wouldn't try to write it himself—or anything else ever again, for that matter."

Owen snorted. " 'Based upon.' Nothing but a screen-writing legalism. If I tell you a story, Charlotte, and you go home and write a book about it, where's my gripe? After all, I could have kept my mouth shut and written it myself. Still could, in fact, since the book you wrote wouldn't be the same book I'd write—look how many times the Grimms' fairy tales have been retold, for heaven's sake."

"So you do think Bell might at least have gotten the idea for *Harlan's Heart* from Fischer?"

Owen leaned his huge bulk against the doorframe and sighed. "Lord, here I am defending the man I'll go to jail for murdering. But the thing is, Charlotte, it's not just a matter of plot, or even the theme or ideas in the book. Boy goes to big city, makes good—that's all old hat, we've all read that a million times. But to steal the thing that made *Harlan's Heart* what it was—what it is—well, that's just entirely different."

He waved his big hands helplessly. "You read it, Charlotte, you'll see what I mean. The language, the rhythm of the prose—hell, the damned thing reads like it's written in fresh blood."

He shook his head, whether in awe or envy I could not tell. "And to steal *that*," he said, "he'd have had to be even worse than everyone who knew him agreed he was."

The big hands dropped. "To steal that," he finished, "Wes Bell would have had to be a vampire."

"I REALLY DO wish you hadn't let him, that's all."

It was 10 PM, and I'd just learned where my children were. Joey, I mean, and Myron Rosewater whom Solli had given permission to go downtown, alone, to a rock concert at the Coliseum.

"Charlotte," Solli said patiently, placing a pillow under my feet and handing me a glass of club soda, "he'll be perfectly all right. I sent them in a cab and they'll be taking one home when the concert's over. What could happen?"

"All kinds of bad things." Irritably I fiddled with the television remote, turning to the local news to see if any bad things had. "They could have a riot or a fire in that place, and Joey could get stuck in an aisle or knocked out of his chair and not be able to escape. Myron's just not responsible enough to be taking—"

"Myron," Solli said, "would step in front of an eighteen wheeler for Joey, and you know it. Harry Lemon was supposed to go but he couldn't, so at the last minute he gave Joey the extra ticket and I said it was okay. So if he comes home in a sack I guess it's all my fault, but I'm telling you he'll be just fine."

He lifted my head, sitting down on the sofa where I was lying, then lowered my head onto his knee. "He's not a cripple, Charlotte, he just can't work his legs.

There's a difference, but we could convince him there isn't if we aren't careful."

"I could, you mean," I replied miserably. "I mean, I know you're right—the way I watch him and protect him, and try never ever to let even the slightest little thing bad happen to him. I'll turn him into Caspar Milquetoast."

Solli's knee moved as he laughed. "I doubt that. Joey's a tougher kid with no working legs than most kids are with two; I'll bet he can survive your mothering him. But you've got to let him do the things an ordinary sixteen-year-old kid does, like jumping up and down with a lot of other sixteen-year-olds, yelling his lungs out and getting all caught up in the herd instinct."

"Getting all sweaty and overheated, you mean, and chilled half to death afterwards."

Still, I supposed that Solli was probably right. On the television screen now was a picture of a woman who had gone out to buy a new roll of dental floss and gotten caught in a robbery attempt. She was not expected to live. Next came the film of a smoldering DC-10, one of whose engines had sucked in a flock of seagulls, and finally the story of a man who'd been walking down a street, peacefully minding his own business, when a piece of ventilation grating collapsed and he fell a dozen feet onto the subway tracks below where the Seventh Avenue express ran over him.

All of which only supported Solli's real argument: you could run but you couldn't hide, and if you couldn't run you still couldn't hide. If Joey was going to live he had to risk getting hurt, and if I was going to live I had to let him.

Nevertheless I finished watching the news just to make sure the Coliseum's roof hadn't fallen in or the National Guard been called out, and they hadn't. Solli got up to fetch me another glass of soda and to get his laptop word processor, on which he was composing a piquant little essay about suturing blood vessels so they do not later twist up into useless knots of a spaghetti-like substance, and after a while I picked up *Harlan's Heart*.

"Solli," I said, stopping in the middle of page ten, "if we ever broke up and then I wrote a novel and put you in it, only I left out all your good parts and put in the awful parts, and I made the awful parts terribly awful and also terribly funny and on top of that I made you completely recognizable—"

"Mmph," Solli said, typing. "Couldn't be done. I don't have any awful parts."

"Hmm. I have to admit you have a point, there. But if you did and I did and they were, would you—"

Solli looked up from the laptop screen. "Were what?" he asked, charitably not pointing out that by interrupting him I had just set vascular surgery back a good fifteen years or so.

"Awful," I said, "and funny, and recognizable. If I put you in a book that way, would you kill me?"

"Oh," he said, returning his gaze to the laptop. "Nope. I'd just let you die of remorse. Anyway, nobody I know reads fiction except me. They're all too busy reading up on how much levophed it takes to blow out a lab rat's left ventricle, and other good stuff like that. So it'd probably be a waste of time putting me in there in the first place. Why, were you thinking of it?"

"No." I frowned down at *Harlan's Heart*. "Just wondering. Because so far this book reminds me of those rituals they still do in primitive tribes, some places. They take a really sharp blade and cut designs into a person, and then rub salt and ashes in the open flesh so the wounds can never heal right. It's meant to hurt, you see, and the scars are supposed to last forever."

"Sort of the opposite of what I do."

"Uh-huh. And in this book, Wesley Bell did it to a critic he knew, this Phileta Poole. Only he called her Phyliss Philpot, and she may be the dumbest, vainest, horniest, greediest, and most undiscriminating literary critic ever written into English prose. And she's absolutely hilarious, only I'll bet she didn't think so."

He shrugged. "Yeah, but if she wanted to knock him off it sounds like she'd have had to take a number. From what you've been telling me, it seems more and more like his personality was a serious hazard to his health."

"You've got that right," I said, re-reading the part where Phyliss Philpot lures the struggling young genius novelist up to her apartment, which is full of old cat food cans, cat droppings, and cats, and tells him she'll only give his first novel a good review if he gives her a good...well, anyway, it was funny, especially the part about the skin-diving outfit. Funny, and extremely cruel.

"I wonder why I never got his *Pen and Pencil* stuff for this issue," I mused, putting the book aside for the moment. "Maybe he'd just been waiting until I got good and dependent on him, so when he stiffed me it would really hurt."

I sat up as a burst of enlightenment came over me; the book fell to the floor. "Or maybe not."

Just then I heard a car pull up in front of the house. It was not, I thought as I peered out, a taxicab—not unless taxis were now painted candy-apple red and came equipped with glass packs, funny-car suspension, and a horn that went ooh-*ooh*-gah! and then played the shark theme from *Jaws*.

"I thought," I said to Solli, "you told them to come home in a cab."

"Mmm, probably they ran into some friends, got a ride," he said unconcernedly, not looking up from his work.

"That's not the point. This point is, you *told* them—"

"Man, those guitars were wicked," Myron Rosewater enthused from the vestibule. "And how'dja like that drummer guy, that Boss Waxman from the Screamin' Meemies? Man, I like to get me a big tattoo like that."

"Yeah," said Joey, "but you'd have to get yours in white or it wouldn't show up. I could get one, though," he added quite a lot more thoughtfully and seriously than I liked. "Maybe on my shoulder, a nice big dragon with fangs," he finished as they came on into the living room.

"Hey, guys," said Solli, his fingers still calmly moving on the laptop's keyboard. "How was the concert?"

"Wow, it was great," said Joey. His eyes looked glassy and feverish, his face unnaturally flushed. His shirt was soaked through with sweat and his hair was plastered to his head, and although the night was cool Solli had apparently not thought to make him wear a sweater. Also, his breath smelled of beer.

"Myron," I said pleasantly, "since you didn't bother to follow Dr. Solli's instructions about taking a cab home, perhaps you'd like to return the money he gave you for it."

Myron looked uncomfortable. "Uh, yeah. Well, uh, it's a funny thing about that. I'll pay you back, Dr. Solli. But see, what happened was..."

"What happened was, someone in that ridiculous vehicle you rode home in was old enough, or looked old enough, to buy beer. And you gave them the taxi money to buy it, isn't that right?"

Myron frowned at his shoes.

"And you," I said, turning to Joey, "drank some of the beer, which you have been expressly forbidden to do unless you are home here in my presence or with Solli."

"I only took one swallow. I was thirsty." Joey glanced at Solli in hopes of reinforcement, a tactic that served only to increase my anger at all three of them.

"You," I said to Joey, "are grounded until further notice, and you," I turned to Solli, "are not to give permission for Joey to do anything or go anywhere without checking it with me first."

"And you," I told Myron, "will go straight home and explain to your mother why you were out riding around in a carful of kids who had beer and then you are to have her call me, unless you want me to call her and tell her about it, the results of which I guarantee you will not like one bit. Do I make myself clear?"

"Hey, Miss Kent," Myron began, spreading his hands in the falsely-placating let's-cool-down-the-old-lady manner that always makes me want to swat him.

"Come on, Charlotte," said Joey in the I-can't-*believe*-this tone he occasionally uses to test the limits of my patience.

"I think," said Solli in his mildest let's-not-get-excited-about-this voice, "if we simply discuss this in a reasonable—"

"The discussion," I said, "is closed. Although if you want to open it again we could talk about a few other rules that seem to be getting short shrift around here lately, such as the one that says curfew is 9 PM on school nights and it is now 11:45, or the one that says when a person winds up doing all the cooking she should not also wind up doing all the shopping, and I notice that we are out of bread and almost out of milk, and if there is no coffee left for me to make tomorrow morning I am going to be mightily upset."

At this, a sudden recollection appeared to strike Solli; he frowned and got out of his chair.

"You know," he said casually, "I think I'll take a little jog to the convenience store. Come on, Myron, you can go with me as far as Wooster Street. Want anything, Charlotte? Joey?"

"Yeah," Joey muttered, "a new life."

"No, thank you," I told him. "And Myron, don't forget I'm going to be speaking with your mother tomorrow, and if you know what's good for you you'd better make sure you do it first."

"Right," said Myron resignedly, and when they were gone I turned back to Joey for a little reviewing of just exactly what our responsibilities were around here, anyway, and the dialogue that followed was not at all like the conflict which I understand occurs between mothers and teen-agers on television situation comedies.

It was not like anything else I can imagine, either, except possibly World War III, with Joey informing me that if I wanted a helpless infant then maybe I ought to go out and adopt one of those, as just because he happened to get around on wheels did not mean he belonged in a baby carriage, for Christ's sake, and I told him that if that was the kind of language he picked up from people he met at rock concerts then maybe he would be better off not attending any more of them, a circumstance I guaranteed could be readily arranged if I got any more smart talk out of him, and furthermore if he really wanted to live like an adult then just possibly he could start by picking up the dozens and dozens of dirty socks that were strewn around his room, since difficult as it might be for him to comprehend, I did have a few other things I wanted to accomplish in my life besides picking up after him day in and day out as if he were King Tut.

"Fine," Joey said, his voice dripping with the kind of contemptuous venom that only the bodies of boys between the ages of twelve and nineteen are able to manufacture. Furiously he spun himself around and gave his wheelchair wheels a terrific shove, not noticing that his left foot-support had caught itself in a loop of lampcord.

The crash, when it came, was one of those things that make you want to run the tape backwards, fifteen seconds or fifteen years, whatever it takes to undo the damage that has occurred. His foot caught the cord, the cord pulled taut but finally gave in and took the lamp, and as the lamp went over Joey made an attempt to catch it, jerking his body hard to the right while pulling up on the left wheel.

A split second later he was sprawled face-down on the floor with the chair turned over on top of him, pieces of broken lamp spinning on the polished hardwood.

"Joey," I said, scrambling over to where he lay pounding the floor with his clenched fists, "are you all right?"

His face was purple, absolutely purple. Veins bulged on the sides of his neck and forehead. "Get away from me," he sobbed. "Get the fuck away from me, Charlotte, I can do it *myself*."

Clutching onto one wheel he righted the chair; with his arms he hauled his body up into it, facing it. Then in a sort of gymnastic crossover maneuver he balanced on the armrests, his shoulder muscles bulging as he turned and lifted himself, gasping with effort as he lowered himself at last into the leather seat.

"Get out of my face," he bit off the words in a strangled voice, swivelling the chair around and refusing to look at me.

"I'll pick up my fucking socks and I'll earn my own fucking living, too, if I have to—you just keep out of my room and my feelings and out of my goddamned *life*."

FOUR

AS YOU MAY IMAGINE, the rest of Tuesday night was pretty quiet, but on Wednesday morning I woke to a silence so deep and luxurious it took me a moment before I realized how wrong it was.

No whistling from Solli, who on most days feels it necessary not only to rise with the birds but to imitate them as well. No hissing of the shower in Joey's bathroom, no twangs or shrieks or moans of what he fondly believes is music coming from his stereo. Not even any sounds out of the kitchen, where by now a series of clinks, clatters, and crashes should have been signalling attempts at breakfast preparation.

Alarmed, I glanced at the clock which said 8:45, although of course I knew that had to be wrong too since anyone in this house who could sleep past 6:30 was either deaf or brain-dead. Pulling on my robe I padded down the hall barefoot, as generally the only time I can locate my slippers is when I am already wearing them, and found Joey's door standing open.

He wasn't there. Also, his room was clean: bed made, dresser top tidied, books lined up in the bookcase, and shoes in the shoe rack. Even his laundry hamper had been emptied, a project I had been sternly reminding myself to undertake as soon as I obtained the necessary equipment—rubber gloves, plastic apron, and a gas mask—and there was not a single dirty sock in evidence.

"Joey?" I whispered, peering into his closet.

From the basement I could hear a steady squeak-and-rumble, as of heavy demolition equipment being operated in the distance, that signalled Helen's decrepit old washing-machine going into its unsteady spin cycle while the dryer labored over its task of whirling partly-cleaned clothing in a stream of partly-warmed forced air.

Helen, of course, had never done a shred of laundry in her life; still I thought that before she returned we really ought to buy her a brand-new washer and dryer, since the amount of dirty wash generated by one teen-aged boy in a single day was enough to make even the *Maytag* man weep, and sometime in her privileged life Helen might want to run a load of lace hankies or something.

As I neared the kitchen I heard a less familiar sound which I finally identified as National Public Radio's morning music program, a luxury I am ordinarily denied on account of Solli's need for baseball scores in summer, football scores in autumn, hockey scores in winter, and basketball scores, it seems to me, all year round, and after that he likes to hear the traffic report in order to find out how many trauma victims he is likely to encounter when he gets to work.

"Solli?" I said, and stopped. On the kitchen table, plunged into a cut-crystal vase that someone had dug out and washed, were a dozen red roses whose perfume mingled sweetly with the smell of coffee. The coffee itself was in a white china pot on a warming-plate, next to a single place-setting of Helen's good silver, a cup and saucer of bone china with a thin gold rim and a pattern of blue forget-me-nots, and a linen napkin someone had found and ironed. Propped against the juice glass was a note:

Dear Charlotte (this part was in Solli's squarish hand), Thought you could use some extra sleep. I have dropped Joey at school & will pick him up after, then take for burgers (unless you call & say not) don't worry about dinner. Will tell Harry L. to eat at own house for change. All OK, see you later, love Solli.

Following this in Joey's Palmer-derived scrawl was: Dear C, Sorry about last night, I am a Big Jerk sometimes. Do Not Finish Laundry!! I will do!!! Look in oven. Love JR.

So I did look in the oven and there was a big plate of hot french toast in there, along with a pitcher of syrup and four sausages burned just the way I like them. I dried my eyes on the linen napkin and sat in the kitchen listening to a Hayden horn concerto, dipping toast in syrup and sipping hot coffee, knowing I was the luckiest woman in the world to be living with a pair of sports-obsessed, medicine-obsessed, rock-and-roll obsessed idiots who could nevertheless figure out how to run a washing machine, make french toast, and buy roses at seven o'clock in the morning all at the same time and all in perfect silence.

And then I got dressed and went after the son of a bitch who killed the poet.

"WHY," I demanded of Lieutenant Michael X. Malley, "would Owen Strathmore beg me for help and then try to scare me off from helping him?"

Malley sat in the small, dingy, smoke-polluted room that the New Haven Police Department likes to call his office, scowling at me from behind the heap of file folders scattered on the scarred, cluttered, terminally depressing grey metal object that he likes to call his desk.

"Because," he growled—the growl being Malley's only known form of communication other than the occasional bellow—"he's a dumb rich loony who thinks he's smarter'n me, that's why."

He peered at me through his pouchy, bloodshot, frighteningly intelligent pale blue eyes. In his left fist he clutched a fat brown cigar whose chewed end resembled something unmentionable in family literature; in his right he gripped a jelly doughnut. He puffed sickeningly on the cigar, laid it with surprising delicacy in what had once been a soup-bowl and was now a truly ghastly ashtray, and finished ingesting the first of many and varied items of junk food he forced into his body during his working day.

Then from a Styrofoam cup he swallowed a gulp of a substance that looked like old crankcase oil and smelled like battery acid, crumpled the cup in his stubby blunt-tipped fingers, tossed the cup at the round file, missed it, and smiled.

At least, on Malley it was what served as a smile.

"That guy no more lives in the freaking normal universe," he said, "than I am freaking Sigmund Freud. I know his type, thinks he doesn't have to live by the normal rules everyone else has to put up with. No, he's a freaking fancy-pants intellectual, got a big house and a shrivelled-up old house-keeper and a bunch of old books fulla goddamn worms, nobody's ever read 'em and nobody ever will. Lives in a freaking tomb, there, typin' out them stories that make all the skinny boys drool an' wet their pants, then run out and load up on firepower.

"Which," he added, "he has done a good job of, himself. You know how much ammo the guy had socked away down there? All kinds, and plenty of it, makings too—shotgun press, brass caps, primer and wadding, powder alone enough to blow the whole block to hell. Plus a half-dozen old World War II grenades, packages of fuse cord, buncha corroded shells lined up on a shelf there, so unstable we hadda call the bomb squad in to move 'em."

He snorted. "Fat freakin' weirdo with a basement like a goddam munitions dump, you're tellin' me he's freakin' harmless? Your problem, you got a soft spot for interesting losers, appeals to your sense of the bizarre, or something. Ask me, guy never met the woman in his life. Just like kinda adored her from afar, you know, wrote a buncha freakin' letters, got himself all hopped up, then he goes and blows away the husband, you know? Classic."

"Ammo?" I repeated disbelievingly. Malley was wearing his usual tasteful ensemble of yellowed rayon shirt, clip-on red bow tie, and a rumpled plaid sport jacket so loud it could have been used for signalling air-to-ground rescue missions.

His appearance was misleading, however, as usually when Lieutenant Mike Malley thought somebody dunnit they had, and usually he found them and caught them and got them convicted for doing it, too.

"You ever known the guy to have any other girlfriends?" he demanded. "Have what you call a social life, any of the normal back-and-forth?"

"Well, no," I admitted, forbearing to mention that as far as I knew Malley didn't either. "But you still haven't answered my question. If Owen did it, why would he call me?"

"He didn't call you," Malley pointed out with satisfaction. "You called him. First guy you thought of, you said, an' when that happened he figured he'd better play it real cute, pretend like someone's tryin' a put the finger on him.

"Which," he finished grimly, "I am, an' I'm gonna. So why don't you go on home an' play with that magazine of yours, Cut an' Paste or whatever the hell it's called, let me do my freakin' work, here. An' don't worry about Strathmore playin' any more tricks—I'm watchin' him so hard, I got guys countin' his nose hairs. He scratches his rump, I'll have a color picture of it."

Malley pointed a stubby tobacco-stained finger at me. "Guy's got a motive, the gun, the chance, an' you're involved with him. What else do I need to tell me he's a freakin' nut case?"

"Helen wasn't a nut case," I pointed out, and Malley's scowl grew more ferocious. Not too long ago he'd been ready to arrest her for murder, too, and if I hadn't been around he would have. He looked like a

pit bull, had the temperament to match, and now that
he'd sunk his choppers into Owen I would have to find
something infinitely more attractive and wave it right
in front of him, before he would even think about letting go.

"Yeah, that was the exception that proves the rule.
Now go on, I ain't got time to play cop games with
you."

I waited, but he didn't say anything more. He
didn't, for instance, tell me to mind my own damned
business, or threaten to lock me up and throw away
the key on charges of obstruction or interfering or any
of the other penny-ante offenses he'd tried arresting
me for and even locking me up for in the past, in his
fruitless but determined efforts to keep me out of his
face.

And that, I thought as he lit up the awful cigar
again, was perhaps the most interesting thing I had
learned from Malley so far. He wanted someone for
Bell's murder and the poet's, all right. He wanted it
the way a pit bull wants a juicy steak, and there was no
way I was going to keep him from getting it.

But he also didn't care whose haunch the steak got
carved from. He'd bite anything warm and bloody, as
long as it smelled right. If I brought him a tastier
chunk of lunch meat than the one on his plate, his
unusual silence told me, he would drop what he was
gnawing in favor of a new, more toothsome morsel.

By not telling me not to, the only thing he could be
doing was inviting me to. And although I couldn't help
wondering why, it did make a very pleasant change in

our relationship, sort of like the change that occurs when the dentist stops drilling on your tooth.

"Why, Lieutenant Malley," I said wonderingly, "am I to infer that you actually have some measure of confidence in me?"

"Yeah," he growled, puffing out a choking cloud of cigar smoke, "I got confidence you can get your butt in a sling. Now scram out of here, I mean it. Don't come back unless you got something useful to say, which I figure means probably never."

Musingly, I went out the door and through a larger room full of crooks, con men, muggers, chain-snatchers, dope sellers, dope addicts, and dopes. As I did, it dawned on me that Michael X. Malley might have some reason for not coming down on me at once like a ton of poorly-loaded construction material.

Such as that he wasn't expecting me to deliver him another suspect but to deliver Owen himself, who after all was not languishing in a jail cell right this minute.

Malley didn't want any trial that couldn't be prosecuted with the utmost confidence. He liked his murder cases open-and-shut, with special emphasis on the shut part. Furthermore, he thought the community of writers—which I always think of as being much like a community of piranha, but never mind, even homicide cops have their illusions—would talk to me more readily than they would talk to him. And that, of course, was what he wanted to have happen.

He didn't quite like the smell of what was on his plate; if he had, he'd have devoured it already. He'd have found some way to block Owen's getting out on bail. My mission, should I choose to sucker into it, was to waft away the lingering aroma of doubt that was somehow spoiling Malley's appetite.

If I could only figure out what was producing that aroma, maybe I could follow the smell to the stinker. In doing that, I might also get Owen transformed from USDA prime choice back into the ordinary harmless eccentric weirdo I knew he was.

Or at least the one I hoped he was. The weapons collection didn't bother me too much; after all, Owen was already compulsive about collecting books, and writing them. Any other hobby he acquired he was likely to be fairly intense about, too, in the same way that some people pack their houses with old newspapers and odd bits of string, and others sit around and sew buttons on themselves.

The ammunition was something else again, though, and the black powder and fuse cord I didn't like one bit, since as far as I knew there was nothing collectible about black powder and the only use for fuse cord was to make black powder explode.

The more I thought about it the unhappier I got, in fact, because a guy who has the ingredients for one kind of bomb might just possibly also have on hand the makings—and the ability—to create another. One made of springs and a plastic bag of red ink, for instance.

Finally, Owen's gun-room was built of concrete blocks, and although it had not meant much to me at the time I now recalled seeing quite a few of them stacked in a corner of his basement.

Out on the street I breathed in a lungful of what in New Haven is euphemistically described as air: the heady mixture of sun-drenched hydrocarbons and oil-slicked low tide that always sets my pulse to racing and my brain to percolating. Someone had painted a big red "X" on Owen's backside and labeled it "lay blame here," and the why of that was already quite obvious: his affair with Corinna, real or imagined, plus his unusual life-style and collection of weapons made him the perfect fall guy. Even I could see how and why he might have killed Bell. What I didn't get was why Owen—or someone else—would kill the poet. But then suddenly I did. Get it, I mean. The concrete block had not been meant for the poet. It had been meant for me.

RIDING THE Metro-North train into Manhattan is one of those activities that can be enjoyed in recollection or in anticipation but cannot be enjoyed in experience. The seats on the train, for one thing, are orange molded plastic, which would not be so bad except that they were molded to fit some species of passenger other than the human.

The windows, made of a substance I imagine once was clear, are shatterproof, so that when poor tenement-dwelling snipers are moved quite naturally to fire at the heads of the rich Fairfield County suburbanites going by like so many ducks in a shooting gallery, the resulting deaths will be only as a result of flying bullets and not from flying shards of window glass.

The view from these windows alternates between burnt-out abandoned automobiles, overflowing trash dumpsters, and the sort of secluded, litter-strewn areas of weeds and small trees that look as if they are just waiting for the bodies of serial-murder victims to be found half-buried in them.

Finally, the train itself stops at every spot where three or more people have ever been known to gather, including the raised 125th Street platform in Manhattan, where reasons for gathering include most of the major felonies and all of the misdemeanors.

At last however it enters the tunnel to Grand Central Station, passing through an enormous underground railyard stretching like some mythic smoky shadow-world: dull red beacons and sulfurous signal lamps, black encrusted passageways blocked by heaps of tattered cloth that might be the nests where human beings sleep or might be the beings themselves, and always the sense that something more is out there just out of sight where the shadows end and the real dark begins, skulking and muttering and creeping.

Or perhaps this was just a reflection of my grim state of mind. Knowing a killer has had a whack at you takes the bloom off the day, in my experience, especially when the person the killer has hit is the sort who used to take the spiders he found in his bathroom carefully outdoors instead of flushing them down the toilet the way any normal heartless unimaginative person would.

I joined the herd plodding up the walkway toward the station proper, between billboards advertising magazines, Scotch whiskey, and Broadway shows. In the vast main room beneath the blue dome all spangled with stars I trudged determinedly through the crowd of mumbling beggars, shambling panhandlers, shuffling bag ladies, and stumbling hebephrenics who seem rapidly to be turning the island of Manhattan into something out of a George Romero film.

By contrast, Phileta Poole's apartment on East 64th Street was like a setting from one of those novels where the brand-names of designer clothes, liquors, and perfumes are the real main characters with the plot and the people merely sketched in as an afterthought, vehicles for consumables in the same way chips are vehicles for dip.

Standing in the crisp black-and-white tiled foyer of her building while the uniformed doorman called upstairs to announce me, I looked around at the waxed oaken wainscoting, lush Boston ferns and onyx vases full of freshly cut lemon lilies and thought that literary criticism had gotten a lot more lucrative since I tried it last. That, or Phileta Poole had another source for her apparently enormous cash flow.

Walking into her apartment confirmed my impression: this wasn't money, this was wealth, the kind that if you wake up one morning and want to become a monk you just go out and buy Tibet. A dozen Irish women had crippled their fingers and ruined their eyesight to make the lace draped casually at the windows. Over the floors spread a silky ocean of rugs: Tabriz, Ming, a dozen more whose intricate hand-knotted patterns I could not identify.

The sofas and chairs were covered in the kind of velvet corduroy that feels like heaven, wears like iron, and costs the earth. On the walls were the sort of unimportant little pictures I gathered Phileta found amusing: a Renoir sketch, a small Pisarro portrait, and a larger oil I thought must be a Monet.

And now I was doing it, I realized: characterizing a person by her belongings. The trouble was that in this case it seemed unavoidable, since Phileta Poole herself—at first meeting, anyway—seemed hardly to be there at all.

"Hello," she whispered, holding out her plump, child-sized hand. Her face was like a small soft dish of vanilla pudding from which her pale grape-green eyes bulged slightly, above a tiny pug nose and lips like an infant's. Her hair, wispy and nothing-colored, had either been hacked at herself or there was a hairdresser somewhere in need of some serious career reevaluation.

Nevertheless beneath that uncertain exterior I sensed a determination that was not uncertain at all, as if she were holding herself together by sheer force of will. Somewhere deep inside Phileta Poole, I thought as she gripped my hand with surprising strength, was a tough little pellet of personality refusing against all odds to dissolve.

"Sit down," she invited. "I do appreciate your coming all this way. I've read your book, you know. I thought it was very good." She indicated one of the heavenly armchairs.

"You read Heck of A Deck?" Cautiously, I seated myself; the chair was so soft that for a moment I felt like Alice falling backwards down the rabbit-hole, but then everything stabilized.

"Oh, no." Her laugh was like a sweet pure rivulet of water trickling into a pool. "The other one, the one where you solve the murder."

Her expression grew solemn; she looked down at her clasped hands. "I've been wanting to talk to someone about it, you see. About Wesley's death I mean, only I can't, because—oh, dear."

She looked up; the pale green eyes were brimming with tears. Grimly she brushed them away. "Excuse me, please. I've been ill, and weepiness is part of my convalescence, it seems."

She lifted her chin. "At any rate I was awfully glad when you called, because if by chance you are anything as good as the character you wrote about—"

"I'm not," I interrupted her firmly. "No more than you are as bad as the character Bell wrote about. Unless of course you really are like Phyliss Philpot, only just terribly well disguised?"

A pink flush crept from the collar of her plain white blouse, which she wore over a wraparound denim skirt, stockings and penny loafers. "No," she said, "I'm not. At least, I'm not any more."

A movement in the corner of my eye made me turn to a pair of oaken panel doors, just as a tall muscular woman in a navy-blue pants suit stepped between them into the room. Her crepe-soled utility shoes made no sound on the carpets as she strode toward us.

"I didn't realize you had a visitor, Phileta." Her tone implied that she most definitely ought to have known. Phileta had let me in herself.

She was about thirty-five with large smart eyes whose color was the blue of icebergs. Her dark straight hair was cropped bluntly just above her unpierced earlobes, and her skin had the start of that leathery, thickened look that comes from lots of sun exposure: skiing, I thought, or possibly mountain-climbing. No makeup, no jewelry but for a Timex wristwatch professionally equipped with a second-hand.

"Miss Kent," said Phileta too brightly, "this is Miss Brill. My . . . assistant."

"How do you do," I said. "Phileta has been explaining how I can get my book reviewed in some of the larger publications."

I could almost feel Phileta letting out a relieved breath, but Miss Brill did not appear convinced.

"How interesting." Her gaze flicked over me with all the friendliness of a bullwhip. "And what is your book about?"

"Oh, I'm afraid it's not written yet," I replied, "but one must plan ahead, mustn't one?" Then I tittered ineffectually.

"Indeed." Miss Brill looked from me to Phileta and back at me again, as she tried to decide whether I could be as harmless an idiot as I seemed.

"Miss Brill, I wonder if we might have coffee?" Phileta pressed her palms wistfully together like a small child making a wish, then noticed her own gesture and parted them again.

"And some sandwiches," she added more firmly. "Miss Kent, wouldn't you like a sandwich?"

"Oh, well," I hesitated, "if you're sure it's not too much trouble." I'd never been fed sandwiches by a hostile Amazon before; probably it would prove interesting. I smiled at Miss Brill, intercepting the briefest look of long-suffering on her face as she strode off to fix refreshments.

"How did you know?" Phileta asked when she was gone.

"When I see a guard," I replied, "I assume someone is being guarded. And since I was not kept out, I gather the guard is to keep you in."

"Yes, well." Her small soft chin came up defiantly again. "It's not quite what you think. Whatever authority Brill has, I've given it to her. I still need . . . a little help governing my impulses, you see. My drug-seeking impulses," she added, making herself say it. "I'm a recovering heroin addict."

I must have looked surprised; she caught my eye and smiled with genuine friendliness.

"Don't look so amazed. It's easy, becoming a dope fiend—in fact, I think now that was probably most of the attraction."

She shook her head ruefully. "My tenth birthday party was a shooting safari in Africa. Thirty of the children of my father's richest friends, and I don't know how many servants. That was nothing, though, compared to my twelfth birthday—for that one he gave me an insurance company."

I must have made a sound; she smiled at me. "Ridiculous, I know. But then Daddy made the mistake of sending me to the most expensive women's college he could find, which at the time was...well, you know the type I mean. Stream of consciousness poetry is a team sport there, along with pottery and meditation."

Her smile turned amused and I saw the girl that she had been then, the kind some people call "bubbly."

"And at college," she went on, "I learned some things that weren't in the course catalogue, like how to skin-pop cocaine with a diabetic needle and how to go slumming for guys who keep Lucky Strike packs tucked in their rolled-up t-shirt sleeves."

I blinked. If anyone didn't seem the type it was Phileta.

"Also," she added, "I found out I could write. Only I'd never learned how to finish anything—I'd never had to. One of the hired help would always finish things for me at home.

"So I became a critic, and came to New York and lived like a whore," she said with only the barest trace of bitterness. "A rich, spoiled, arrogant critic who put down other people's work because I could never figure out how to do my own."

It was painful listening to her rip herself up one side and down the other. "You're too hard on yourself," I said. "I've read your stuff. It's insightful, and fair."

Her shoulders moved slightly. "Thank you. But you haven't read my later pieces or you wouldn't say so."

She rummaged in the cushion of her chair, found a cigarette and lit it, dropping the match into a blue-and-white porcelain vase that was only about ten centuries old.

"I was good at first, that's true, and it's wrong to pretend otherwise. If I hadn't been, I wouldn't have gotten the reputation I had, would I, or the assignments? There aren't any fools writing for the *TLS*, or the *New York Review of Books*. Well," she amended gently, "I suppose there are some, but I wasn't one of them. And I only partied—" she gave the word a wry twist—"on week-ends."

She paused, remembering. "And then?" I asked.

Phileta came back to herself with a little start. "And then I woke up one Monday morning and needed a hit, needed it like I needed oxygen. That had never happened before, I always said I could take it or leave it alone, but I didn't waste time worrying about it that day. I was too sick to worry, I just went out and found something to get well, just to feel human again. And from then on," she finished softly, "I wasn't doing the hard stuff any more. From then on, the hard stuff was doing me."

It was among the simplest, straightest, least self-pitying descriptions of personal disaster I'd ever heard, and Phileta delivered it as if she were narrating a travelogue: if this is Thursday, we must be in hell. My respect for her went up a notch.

"And what happened next?"

She stubbed out the cigarette. "The standard downhill slide, gradual at the beginning and steep at the end. People still wanted a good word from me, of course, only what they had to do to get it changed because I changed. To get a favorable review from the new Phileta Poole, it wasn't important to be inspired at the typewriter. All you had to be was inspired in bed, with me, and at my command. All those pretty boys who thought they were novelists—and some who really were—I ran them through their tricks like circus animals."

She glanced up, saw my skepticism, rose and crossed to an antique cherry bureau, pulling something from the back of a drawer.

"This is me, a year ago. A friend took it, for a joke."

The snapshot showed a wire-thin young woman with short spiky hair, eyes like coals, and a smile that was utterly predatory.

It was Phileta, all right. As the camera's shutter tripped she was in the act of sticking a needle in her arm, and from the look of anticipatory bliss smeared across her face I figured whatever the syringe was loaded with it probably wasn't vitamins.

"Jesus," I said. "So that's why you couldn't sue him."

"Yes. Every word he wrote about me was true. Only—"

Sounds from the next room signalled the approach of the dreaded Brill. "And how many press releases do you recommend I send out?" I inquired as the woman entered with a tray.

"Oh, as many as you can," Phileta replied. "There's no such thing as bad publicity, you know," and I thought I saw Brill wince.

"Remember," Brill said, sounding like a gym teacher I once had, before I gave up exercising anything but my opinions, "your father is coming at four o'clock."

"Yes, Miss Brill," said Phileta meekly, looking at her lap. Not until we were alone again did she resume speaking.

"Anyway, in addition to Brill there's another motive for me to stay straight," she said. "To make a long story short, my income is from a trust. My name is on things, but my father still signs all the papers and doles out the money."

Dimly I remembered the name of Philip Poole, who if I was not mistaken owned enough hotel rooms to shelter the population of China, along with quite a lot of other things.

"And he's taking an interest, I gather, in your recovery process now?"

She laughed without amusement. "That's putting it mildly. Of course, I'd kept him from finding out what my life was like back then. If he had he'd have absolutely gone crazy. And then I don't know why, but I started cleaning up a little. Mentally, at any rate. Maybe it was all the reading, or maybe it was the writing. You hammer out enough words, you get in danger of believing them."

Phileta shook her head. "Or," she added sadly, "of wanting to believe them. I really think I might have gotten straight by myself, but it was too late. I never got the chance to try."

"Bell's book came out. *Harlan's Heart*. And your father read it."

She nodded. "And he did go crazy. One morning I woke up and there were men in my apartment. They were from him, and they bundled me off for what they said was a vacation."

"And?" I asked, although I knew the answer.

"And," Phileta replied, "that was six months ago, and I got out two weeks ago. I suppose I ought to be grateful to him."

She didn't sound grateful, though. Thinking of this, I felt my emotions warring with my common sense: he'd saved her life. But he'd robbed her of the chance to save it for herself.

"Phileta," said Miss Brill sharply; I hadn't heard her come in. "I really think it's time for your rest, don't you? I'm sure you understand, Miss Kent."

I looked at Phileta, who carefully refrained from hurling her cup as she rose. It occurred to me she wasn't quite as much the source of Brill's authority as she liked to think. Probably for instance she did not sign Miss Brill's paychecks; whoever did would have the final say on what Phileta was or was not allowed to do.

Phileta's next words confirmed this. "I guess I'd better talk fast, Miss Kent, before my assistant here decides I ought to be packed off for another 'vacation.' I hated Wes Bell. I'd never done anything to him to make him write what he did. He wasn't a pretty boy. Maybe," she added, "that was why he did it."

Brill stepped forward; Phileta backed away from her. "I'll never know if I could have gotten better on my own. Wes took care of that, didn't he?"

Her voice dropped defeatedly. "Good book, though, you have to admit that much. A real honest-to-god page-turner. I hear the woman who played me in the movie is in drug rehab now, too. Only," she finished with deep bitterness, "*she* got to decide to go, on her own. I don't even have that much satisfaction."

She turned back to me with a look of desperate appeal. "And I hated him for it, I *still* hate him. That's why I have to talk to someone, you see, about—"

"Phileta," Brill put in warningly. "We needn't burden Miss Kent with our personal problems. That would hardly be polite."

Politeness, I felt sure, had nothing to do with it. But the effect of Brill's reproof on Phileta was like a slap; straightening, she regained at once the inward control I'd sensed earlier.

"Yes," she said, "of course Miss Brill is right. This is a social visit, not a therapy session. Forgive me, Miss Kent, as I told you earlier I'm not quite myself yet. I tend to ramble on."

She put out her hand; as I took it I felt once more the remarkable strength in the small pale fingers.

At the same time something wordless passed between Phileta and Brill; some mingling of caution, apology and acknowledgment I could not even begin to fathom. It was clear that Phileta, not Philip Poole, had captured the Brill woman's loyalty—along, I thought, with her friendship.

"But Miss Brill," Phileta added with a twinkle of unexpected mischief, "while I go and lie down, why don't you give our guest some of that wonderful lemon cake that's in the kitchen? There's too much of it for us to finish, and she has such a tedious trip ahead of her. Don't you, Miss Kent?"

Despite being full of sandwiches, I managed to look suitably eager to try the lemon cake. Meanwhile Brill knew when she was beaten, as she could hardly now refuse what Phileta had offered.

"What a fine idea," she said. "Come along, Miss Kent."

THE KITCHEN was large and antiseptic and equipped with enough appliances to furnish a French cooking school.

"How accurate an historian is Phileta?" I asked frankly. It seemed foolish to keep up my earlier facade; Brill, I felt certain, had taken my measure in the moment she first saw me. She knew it wasn't advice I was after.

She poured out fresh coffee, set slices of lemon cake on plates, and sat across from me at the counter. "The details of her addiction are accurate," she said, "but her belief that she could have helped herself is not. I wish it were—it would make a big difference in the way she feels now."

I felt no compunction over asking about Phileta's personal life; it was, after all, why Phileta had sent us off together. Now Brill apparently felt she might as well be straight with me; feed me a few spare facts along with the lemon cake and send me off—she hoped—satisfied.

"She doesn't remember how bad she was in the weeks before she went to the hospital," Brill went on, poking at the cake with her fork-tines. "Her weight upon admission was eighty-four pounds, and she had a large number of common body parasites as well as a nasty fungal infection."

"And she was committed against her will?"

She nodded. "There was little choice. She would have died within weeks, a few months at most, otherwise."

"And now you care for her, and...curb her impulses?"

Brill looked sharply at me. "You're really not as silly as you were pretending, are you? At any rate, I work for Phileta's father. I'm a psychiatric nurse and he's got others just like me, to watch her around the clock. So why are you really here?"

Not precisely like her, I thought as I told her about my inquiries into Bell's death and the poet's.

I didn't mention Owen Strathmore, though. Something just made me think it might be better not to, like for instance the vision of Poole's men bursting unannounced into a private residence, snatching a woman and taking her where he told them to take her, simply because that was what he was paying them to do.

A guy like that, I make it a rule not to show him all my cards, and I don't flash them in front of the hired help, either, no matter how basically decent they might seem to be. "Has she really been under observation for every single minute?"

Miss Brill moved uncomfortably in her chair. "Of course she has. That is, not my own observation. But someone is always here. She wants it that way. If not, she might lapse back to her old habits and hook up with her old..."

She stopped, frowning at her plate.

"All her old friends," I finished for her, "unsavory friends who know she's got money and might do her a favor if she promised them enough?"

Miss Brill shook her head. "That's ridiculous."

I got up. "Then you won't mind my discussing the theory with a friend of mine, a New Haven homicide detective. He's fond of ridiculous theories, since they so often turn out to be true."

Her cup clinked unsteadily in its saucer. "Please don't do that. The business of Bell being killed has upset her a great deal, that's all. She didn't have anything to do with it."

Not *couldn't* but *didn't*; interesting. I thought about the strength I'd sensed in Phileta. "She's not psychiatrically ill, then, not clinically unstable at all?"

Brill shook her head firmly again. "Absolutely not. She is simply trying to reconstruct herself from some rather ugly ruins. Doing rather a brave and admirable joy of it, too. And..."

"And what?"

"And *while* she does," Brill said, "I earn the generous salary Philip Poole pays me, which I need for...well, never mind. The thing is, if he finds out you got up here I'll lose this job and probably won't get another. He's a powerful man, you know—it doesn't do to thwart him."

"I see. In that case, let's make a deal. Such as, I don't tell anyone anything if you tell me what you're holding back. *Or* I report to Poole on the talk I've just had with his daughter."

I waited, and after a moment she gave in. "Phileta did slip out," she confessed. "Late Sunday afternoon."

"I see." The afternoon, in other words, before Wes Bell was killed. "And then what happened?"

Brill looked uncertain. "You do promise absolutely that you won't tell anyone this."

I took a deep breath. For all I knew, Brill was about to confide that when Phileta was not out blowing away the authors of best-sellers, she spent her time mincing harmless old ladies up in their bathtubs. But if I didn't promise Brill wasn't going to tell me, and then I wouldn't know.

"I won't talk to anyone," I assured her.

She nodded reluctantly. "All right. We nurses were all in a panic, but she came back on her own, Monday afternoon. Minus her earrings—diamond solitaires."

"That's it? You don't know where she'd been?"

"No. She refuses to discuss it. And even if she would—"

"You're not sure you would believe her?" I guessed.

Brill sipped coffee while she considered how to reply. When she did speak, it was judiciously and reluctantly.

"Miss Kent, Phileta is by nature an extremely private person who has for some time now been obliged to live in a restrictive—and personally intrusive—environment. Rehab doesn't only deprive you of your drugs; it also deprives you of your secrets."

"So?" I swallowed some coffee; it was getting cold. As I did so Brill's glacial eyes met mine, warning me not to read more into what she was about to tell me than was really there.

"So," she said, "I think she slipped out simply to have a secret again. Just to be able to have one—

something of her own, something private that no one else knows—that's important to her now. And yes, I do think she would lie to preserve that secret, no matter how harmless it was, just to regain some more control over her own life.''

I got up. My slice of lemon cake lay untouched; Brill's also remained uneaten, reduced to a heap of crumbs by the probing of her fork.

"Confiding secrets is a luxury, too," I said, "and you know, I have the strangest feeling she might have been about to tell me she killed Wesley Bell."

Brill waved the remark away impatiently. "Ridiculous," she said again. "Probably she wishes she had. Naturally she's still very angry with him, as who of us would not be? But wishing and doing are two different things, Miss Kent."

Sometimes yes; sometimes no. It was, after all, her impulses that Phileta had said she still needed help controlling.

But moments later as I stepped from her building out into the bright, bustling freedom of East 64th Street, I found myself hoping intensely for Phileta's sake that Miss Brill was right.

FIVE

RETURNING TO New Haven from Manhattan is like recovering from the plague only to be stricken with a stomach virus. Conditions downtown have gotten so grim and futile lately that workers who perform even the most minor services for the public may almost be forgiven for their attitude, which is that you ought to be grateful you are getting any service at all, never mind how surly, corrupt, or inefficient.

The cab I took from the station had no springs, no muffler, and as far as I could determine no brakes; careening wildly around corners and through red lights it hurtled across town like some renegade missile while the driver alternately cackled and cursed. At last he stopped the vehicle by the ingenious method of turning off its ignition while scraping its tires for fifty feet or so against the curb in front of Helen's house.

Breathlessly I paid him and tottered inside, where I began to feel a little better. It was only five-thirty, Solli and Joey would not be home for hours, and in the golden glow of a late spring evening the whole place shimmered with the sort of silence I have all but given up hoping for, the kind in which I can take a long hot bath without somebody coming in to ask if I remember where he put the bicycle tools or how many fluid ounces there are in a liter or who wrote that tune, anyway, the one that goes dah-di-dah-*dah*-di-dah.

And of course as I was pouring the bath oil, the telephone rang.

"Charlotte," said Bernie in the hale-fellow-well-met tone he always uses when he has bad news and is hoping to convince me that it is really good news, only very heavily disguised.

"Make it fast, Bernie," I said, "I'm standing naked here."

Personally I do not feel it is an agent's job to convince a writer of anything. Agents, I am certain, have been put on earth to convince publishers of things—like for instance the idea that in order for a book to earn back its advance, it is generally necessary to print more than fourteen copies of it.

"Listen, Charlotte, I just got a funny call. I'm hoping you can tell me there's nothing to this, but..."

Uh-oh. That is the thing about Bernie, and one reason why he still remains my agent. Through uphill and down, whether we are slogging together through the write-for-hire muck or sipping the champagne of a new multiple-book contract from our slippers, Bernie always cuts to the chase.

"Does the name Philip Poole mean anything to you?" Bernie went on. "Because somebody from his outfit thinks you have some information Mr. Poole does not want disseminated."

Right. Like maybe that his daughter was out and about when Wes Bell got murdered, and furthermore that she at least felt she had an excellent reason to want Bell dead.

"I'm familiar with the name," I replied cautiously.

After all there was no sense in frightening Bernie; also, I felt sorry for Phileta and on top of that I liked her a lot. But that didn't mean I was sure she hadn't hired some low-life old buddy of hers to blow Wes Bell's brains out onto my desk-blotter. The old buddy could also have rigged the concrete block; Mike Malley was still working on the how of that.

"Talk to me, Charlotte," Bernie Holloway insisted. "Because in case it's slipped your notice, Philip Poole owns half this town. More to the point, he owns the outfit that owns *Pen and Pencil*, which if I'm not mistaken means also that right now he owns you."

I sat on the floor. The linoleum was chilly but not chilly enough.

"You know," I told Bernie, "this whole situation is really starting to burn my tail. I mean, it's not enough the guy owns hotels, which means he owns the whole economy around the hotels. Now I find out he's got a lock on literature, too? He thinks he can get some snivelling underling to call you up? One phone call, he thinks that's all it takes?"

"Charlotte," Bernie said soothingly, "listen to me, now, I think you should just hold on a second. Mr. Poole does not want his family laundry aired. That's a perfectly normal human wish. He is offering something in return, however."

"Sure, like the golden opportunity not to be kidnapped by a squad of his neckless goons and dumped in a rubber room where I can scribble with blunt crayons for the rest of my life. You go tell Poole he can kiss my—"

"*Charlotte.*" I had never heard that tone from Bernie before. It sounded serious, and it sounded scared.

"I'm listening, Bernie," I told him.

"Good," Bernie said, "because what I'm hearing is not really in the nature of a job offer, Charlotte. Bottom line, what I got from Poole's guy was more like a colonization attempt. As in, you let us take over your impoverished little island nation today, or tomorrow morning we turn it into a radioactive atoll that glows in the dark but doesn't show up on the maps any more."

That's Bernie. When push comes to shove he not only catches the drift accurately, he transmits the major movements of the air currents without hesitation or pause.

"Jesus," I said, wondering suddenly if I had remembered to lock the front door, and if I had whether it would do any good.

"Bernie," I asked, "if I wrote a few pages of something very interesting and faxed it down to you immediately, this evening, would you be there to take it off the machine for me yourself and put it away somewhere? I mean somewhere really secure, like maybe in the secret cabinet behind that big potted plant where you keep the good stuff and the jug of branch water."

A brief moment of silence from Bernie, while he figured out whether his life insurance was really up to date and whether it really would keep his wife, his ex-wife, his girlfriends, and his hordes of children both legitimate and illegitimate in the style to which they had all become accustomed.

"Sure," he said finally, and that in a nutshell was the other thing about Bernie: when you needed him he was there for you.

"Good," I told him, "because that is what I am going to do."

"CRIMINY," said Joey Rosen.

It was eleven o'clock at night, and I had already written up my summary of the past few days' events and taken it down to the all-night copy place on Whalley Avenue, where I faxed it to Bernie.

Meanwhile Joey and Solli had gotten home, cheerfully stuffed with hamburgers and speeding from the processed sugar in all the Cokes they had drunk, and Solli was down in the basement sweating off the excess glucose on the stationary bicycle and listening to the A's game from the coast.

That left Joey, who was no more ready to go to bed than I was ready to send him there, so I put him to work on a stack of *Pen and Pencil* mail after warning him not to smell anything, lick anything, or touch any envelope that appeared unusual.

Now a mess of stuff that looked like purple Kool-Aid was spreading from the sponge he had been using to seal up the return messages, telling people we had gotten their money and that the first issue of their new subscription would arrive soon.

"Solli!" I yelled, and at my tone he came bounding up the back stairs; we wheeled Joey in to the bathroom with his hands stuck stiffly out in front of him and he plunged them under running water.

"I'm okay, I'm okay," he kept saying as the purple stuff swirled down the drain. "See, it's washing off. It's just some kind of water-activated dye or something, from the envelope glue. Some jerk's idea of a joke."

Solli frowned. "You feel all right? Dizziness, blurred vision, headache? Got a funny taste in your mouth?"

I looked at him. Lots of toxins can be absorbed through the skin: weedkillers, insecticides. Even more effective, of course, is putting them in your mouth, and if I hadn't been feeling so presciently paranoid Joey would have been licking the return-mail envelopes shut instead of sealing them with a sponge.

"Yeah," Joey said, looking up into the bathroom mirror, "I'm fine." A look of mischief twinkled in his eyes. "Only... oh, no! My god, I can't walk!"

I sagged against Solli, who squeezed me with one arm while ruffling Joey's hair with the other.

"Take a shower," he told the boy, "with plenty of soap. Scrub off good. And," he said to me, "let's have a look at that envelope."

"Three showers in one day," Joey moaned, but he started stripping off his clothes—a task I was extremely grateful that he had mastered at the heavy-duty four days a week class he went to, called "Advance Life-Skills Rehabilitation" by the physical therapists who run it but dubbed "Weasels on Wheels" by the burly-armed young men who attend it regularly.

Out in the living room we examined the evidence, to not much avail. The subscription data—false, I was quite sure—had been typed with a faded black ribbon on an old manual machine whose keys needed cleaning, which meant it looked just like all the other mail I received from *Pen and Pencil* subscribers except that this was spelled and punctuated correctly. Also it bore no jelly-stains or coffee rings, factors which if I had been handling it would certainly have alerted me, since there is something about an 8-1/2 X 11 sheet of clean white bond imprinted with twenty-five lines of crisp black letter-quality type and a one-inch margin all around that my readers seem to feel is crass.

"Doesn't smell like much," Solli said, cautiously putting his nose near the purple-stained envelope.

"Neither does carbon monoxide," I said. "For god's sake, don't put it in your mouth."

But he had already touched his finger to the tip of his tongue. "Doesn't taste like much, either. Interesting."

Having him fall down writhing in tetanic spasms would be pretty interesting, too, I thought, gazing at him in terror. But he did not fall down and no spasms ensued, and after a while we decided that whatever the purple stuff was, so far it was proving harmless.

"I think Mike Malley should see this," Solli mused, and went out to the kitchen for a plastic bag to put it in.

"I also think," he said when he came back, "that you need to adjust your strategy."

This was a comment that gave me considerable pause, because ordinarily Solli has no nerves. He is the kind of fellow who hops up every morning, eats a hearty breakfast, and tootles off cheerfully to work where he spends his day bushwhacking through the vital organs of other people, most of whom are already only a hair's breadth from the columns of tomorrow's obituary pages.

Ordinarily too he deters them at least for a while from the only fame most of them will ever finagle, a feat about which I have mixed feelings since if I could ever get fifteen minutes of publicity out of my publisher I would almost agree to take it in the form of an obituary.

Still, luckily for his patients Solli's hands do not shake, his voice does not tremble, and his digestion could metabolize pig iron. At the moment however he looked worried, and I doubted it was because he was mentally re-playing the events of his day's final aortic aneurysm repair.

"I think you should accept Poole's offer," he said.

I stared at him. Most of the rest of my conversation with Bernie had consisted of me getting him to agree that he would (A) continue collecting my reports of day-to-day developments in what was turning out to be quite a nasty predicament, and (B) in case the predicament should turn suddenly nastier, resulting in my death or other traumatic inability to use my typing-fingers, deliver the reports to the *Village Voice*, *Rolling Stone Magazine*, the *National Enquirer*, and *TV Guide*, in that order. Before he hung up, however, Bernie had outlined the carrot part of what Philip Poole had in mind, and this I had related to Solli. The stick portion of the program, we gathered, would need to be described only in the event I turned out to need some assistance in figuring which side my bread was buttered on.

"You'd better call the Poison Control Center," I told Solli now. "Whatever that purple stuff was, it's eating out your thought centers."

"Oh, I don't know," Solli said in the mild, reasonable tone he always uses when he is really ripping mad, and if he were not solemnly sworn to do no harm would go out immediately and tear somebody's lungs out. "After all, what he wants is pretty easy."

Easy, and also profitable: a compilation of the best of *Pen and Pencil* magazine, to be published as a mass-market paperback with a raised foil-cover, good distribution, and a long introductory essay by that guy from Maine, the one who sells more scary stories than Nathan's sells hot dogs and who if he wanted to could publish his check-stubs and his laundry lists, that is how hungry his fans always are for something—any-thing—new out of him.

With his name on the cover, *The Best of Pen and Pencil* would sell out before it hit the bookstores, and Poole was offering the standard anthology-editor's compensation deal: half the advance and a percent-age of the royalties, which with the Maine guy also represented inside the book was like a license to print money.

Like most printing jobs too, however, it was dirty, and in this case I didn't think any amount of Boraxo would get the stain off my hands. Simply, it was a bribe to stop my snooping.

"Look," Solli said, "Poole already knows you saw Phileta. Probably he also knows she was AWOL.

Otherwise what would he have to want to shut you up about?''

"Spy in the ointment," I agreed. "Maybe one of the other nurses told him, or he's got someone watching the place from outside. He might even know where she was Sunday night."

I looked at Solli. "Do you suppose he's setting up Owen Strathmore for Wes Bell's murder, to protect her?''

He frowned. "Well, there's no law saying all hotel tycoons are smart. But I wouldn't bet on it. If I were him, I'd be staying as far from all this as possible, keep the deflector shields up and just sit tight. Handle problems as they arise.''

"It's true, he could have had her out of the country by now if he wanted to. And he's being pretty open in his attempts to keep me quiet, isn't he?''

"One big bribe's lots easier to handle than a squad of thugs running around bonking poets and planting evidence and mailing ink-bombs. Which doesn't mean he can't really hurt you if you don't take his offer. You could wake up and find out you're unemployable, except maybe at *The Sawdust Review* in Klamath Falls."

"Blackballed." I shuddered. "You're right, I'll bet he could do that. So that's why you think I should pretend to take the bait? Not because I'm quitting, but so he'll think I am?''

"I think," Solli said, "there is probably not much work for me in Klamath Falls. Also, I don't think you should pretend—I think you should do the book Poole's offering to buy. After all, if you do, you'll need to scout up new material, won't you? Not just old pieces from the magazine, but some fresh stuff?''

Solli is sometimes so brilliantly, marvelously devious, it is all I can do not to fling myself bodily at him in appreciation.

"Besides," he said, "you're always saying the only way to handle a publisher is to take all his money away from him."

"And," I mused, "if I'm scouting new material, it's only natural I'll be scouting it *from* somebody—like maybe from other writers who might have known and hated Wes Bell."

Solli really is about the loveliest creature I have ever laid eyes on, all crinkly blue eyes and straight white teeth and compact, well-conditioned musculature.

"That's my girl," he said, seeing me get the point, "smarter than the average bear."

In the other room Joey's shower hissed off and we heard him moving around, turning his stereo down and snapping on his reading lamp. Finally we heard his bedsprings creaking as he shifted, positioning his legs in the prescribed manner and fixing a foam pad between them so the skin on his knees and ankles would not rub together and break down in pressure sores.

"Night," he called and we called our good nights back to him. Then we began checking doors and turning out lights, making sure everything was shipshape and setting the coffeemaker to start perking bright and early in the morning. Solli checked in with his service one last time while I brushed my teeth, and I turned the sheets back, opened both bedroom win-

dows and lowered the shades while he brushed his.
And *then* I flung myself at him.

"OH, MISS KENT," said the typist doubtfully, "I
don't think I'm very well equipped to—"

"Nonsense," I told her, "you can spell, parse, and
punctuate, which believe me is more than most people can do. And certainly you spend more time in front
of a typewriter than most people do."

"But Miss Kent, I've only been typing what other
people write, not—"

"So, pretend other people wrote this. What's so
hard?"

It was 9 AM and I'd set her up in Solli's study, which
he never uses as he prefers to work in the living room
with the television tuned to the sports channel. The
study was furnished with a roll-top desk, a brass library lamp with a green glass shade, and an electric
typewriter that boasted memory storage, automatic
form-feed paper advance, and a control console that
would probably feel a lot more at home on the flight
deck of a B-52.

"Hmm," said the typist in a manner I would soon
learn to recognize, "I never thought of it that way."
Briskly she began flipping switches and turning knobs;
the typewriter gave a startled little lurch and sprang to
humming life.

"What," she inquired, "is this other person supposed to have written about?" She smiled up from the
keyboard. With her silky yellow-white hair and her
pale blue eyes red-rimmed from weeping for the poet,
she resembled an intelligent albino rabbit.

"Format," I said firmly, thinking that anyway she had more nerve than most rabbits. Working for me—being anywhere near *Pen and Pencil* doings, in fact—was not exactly turning out to be a health kick.

On the other hand she had little alternative, unless she wanted to sign on with an insurance company and die of boredom, or become the worked-to-death "girl" in a one-girl office—a phrase that always makes me think of a moppet in hair-ribbons and a polka-dotted pinafore, perched on the edge of a desk somewhere swinging her Buster Browns and licking a lollipop.

"Format," she repeated, advancing the paper with a flick of her wrist. "How many words, and when do you need them done by?"

I smiled back at her; maybe she wasn't a very experienced professional writer, but she had the professional attitude down pat.

"Two thousand," I said, "by the end of today, if you can. That's eight—"

"I know." She glanced up confidently. "Eight pages—no problem. I type sixty-five words a minute, remember?"

I considered mentioning the fact that writing an essay from scratch is not exactly like copy-typing, then decided I would have to be insane to tell her any such thing since if this girl turned out really to be able to crank out copy at anything even halfway like sixty-five words a minute, my problems were over.

Or at least some of them were over. Thinking of the ones that weren't, I left the typist gazing serenely at an imaginary manuscript, her fingers moving crisply over the keyboard while the paper advanced and words began steadily appearing on it.

"Let's see, now," she murmured: 'You wouldn't show up for an important job interview in shorts and a t-shirt, would you?'"

Ah, the snappy lead-in. Bathed in its reassuring glow I tiptoed from the room, feeling a sensation so unfamiliar it took me a moment to identify it as confidence.

This kid wasn't going to be working in any more insurance companies, or any more one-girl offices either if I had anything to say about it. Other, of course, than in my one-girl office.

So after peeking in on her a final time and finding her engrossed in page two of the article she was quite definitely and purposefully writing, I phoned Reginald Symonds and then headed out to his apartment where I planned to talk him into writing one for me also. And while I was doing that, I would interrogate him about Wes Bell.

Symonds lived in an old four-story building on College Street, way downtown in the shadows of parking garages and the kind of truly ugly monolithic glass-walled office buildings that went from modern to hopelessly retrograde while the contractors were still busy putting in the track-lighting and the inadequate sprinkler systems.

If your field of vision was very narrow, though, you could almost imagine in front of Symonds's building that you were in Cambridge: leaded-glass casement windows that opened screenless outward, a tiny back yard with a tiny herb garden planted in it, old Peugots and Citroens at the curbs. From one of the windows floated a Chopin etude being played swiftly and elegantly on the piano, crisp fast sixteenth-notes of fiendish difficulty mingling with the smells of coffee and roasting chestnuts.

"Come in, come in," said Reggie Symonds heartily, ushering me from the hall in which bicycles were chained. "How nice after all to hear from you. I must say I had a feeling you were not what you appeared to be."

He smiled, exposing an uneven row of tobacco-stained teeth. In bright daylight he looked even older and more motheaten, his moustache droopier and his eyes more watery and defeated. Still he had not abandoned the formalities of entertaining: on his makeshift coffee-table sat a plate of wheatmeal biscuits, a chunk of what looked to be very good cheddar cheese, some fresh grapes, and a pot of tea.

I got the feeling he had dashed right out to buy these items, so I tucked into them with gusto—although not, perhaps, as energetically as I might have had I not suspected they cost him his entire food budget for the coming week.

"So, you want an article from me, hey?" Reggie said, rubbing his hands together at the prospect of an assignment.

He frowned in pretended thought. "I think I can carve out a spot in my schedule, work something up for you. What's it to be about—imagery? Honing the old prose style? Or something a bit more ambitious— say, classical allusions and despair in the late nineteenth century?"

"Reggie, eat a grape. You could use the vitamin C."

His big shaggy head came up alertly, sad eyes spying on me sideways. It was like looking at a very wise old lion in a cage, one who is too tired to maul anymore but could still muster up a solid smack with his heavy paw, if you got too far in his face.

I poured out the tea, dosed his cup heavily with sugar and cream, and handed it to him. I'd been laughing at Reggie and now I felt ashamed; the way his hand shook faintly as he took the cup told me he'd been on short rations quite a while already, and was prepared to endure them for who knew how much longer.

Ah, the carefree existence of the freelance writer: no boss, no time clock. Also no steady paycheck, no health insurance, no pension plan, no paid vacations or holidays, no sick time, and not a shred of job security.

"Let's," I said, "get the business out of the way, all right? I've brought some old issues for you to look at, so you can see exactly the sort of thing I need."

He took the issues and flipped through them—nodding here, frowning there, taking in the whole *gestalt* in thirty seconds.

"How about a piece on copyright law?" he said. "Or one on the tax situation of a part-timer's home office?"

I gazed at him with new appreciation. Reggie at work was quite a different animal from the one who swilled too much free sherry at cocktail parties; sharp, focused, and businesslike. Behind him, one whole wall was covered with reference books: a dictionary of synonyms, a thesaurus, two Bibles, plus swathes more useful subject-specific items. He also had Geberth's brilliantly well-organized and straightforward *Practical Homicide Investigation*; this I thought was an interesting volume for a scruffy old failure like Reggie Symonds to be owning, especially as it looked quite new and I happened to know it cost forty bucks.

The rest of the room was as bare and spare as his larder: an overstuffed chair clearly rescued from the Salvation Army store, a desk made from a hollow-core door and two sawhorses, lampshades and windowshades equally yellow and tattered.

"Fine," I said. "As far as the tone goes, remember your audience. Maybe they're not all going to write the Great American Novel, but our business is to give them what they've paid for—advice that would help them if they ever did write something."

"Or," he added softly, "when they do. It not being my job to decide who gets to try."

His reminder, delivered in the gentlest tone of reproof, made me realize that once upon a time a gangly red-haired kid named Reggie had read magazines just like mine, and for years had done precisely as they advised. He wrote and he rewrote. He studied and scribbled, he practiced and polished. Forsaking all others he pursued the bitch-goddess, trying to get published.

Now in his shabby student-digs apartment, all alone on a low table like a shrine, stood the sum of what he'd gotten for it: six hardcover novels—one, I supposed, every four years for all the time he had been working.

I wondered if he'd ever had a halfway decent review, or a print run of more than three thousand.

"Right," I said, "when they do. And if you decide to take the job." This last of course was merely a sop to Reggie's pride. He needed money: not a fortune, but at once. "Two," I began and his eyes lit up.

"Two articles, three thousand words each, ten cents a word."

"Half," he said mechanically.

"Half," I agreed, "in advance. The rest on Friday, when you deliver the work. Complete. No extensions, no excuses."

A faint look of calculation entered Reggie's eyes; if he'd known I was hurting for the material he'd have tried to hit me up for a higher word-rate. Next time, I saw him thinking.

"Will a check be acceptable?" I opened my handbag. "Or," I proceeded smoothly, "would you prefer cash?"

I'd known the minute I saw his place he was getting the cash, if I had to stand there and stuff it into his pockets myself. So what if his work turned out unacceptable? Poole could afford to sponsor a little grant, help out a starving artist. Besides, I didn't think even the typist could do them all by Friday. I had to have someone else at least trying to write them, and I also needed a way to get Reggie on my side—assuming that he wasn't reading Geberth's *Practical Homicide Investigation* for the purpose of thwarting one, which was another thing I needed to find out.

"Reggie, did you by any chance kill Wesley Bell?"

Symonds's fingers closed around on the wad of twenties I'd had the forethought to pick up from the bank on my way over here. Tucking the bills in his shirt pocket, he leaned forward and cut himself a thick slab of the cheddar cheese. Biting off a chunk he chewed hungrily, swallowed, and washed it down with a gulp of tea.

"Sadly, no," he said. "Good luck to whoever did, though. I would have enjoyed seeing the look on his face, when he realized that someone was about to end his miserable swinish existence."

Well, I hadn't expected him to jump up shouting *mea culpa*.

"Playing a little detective in our spare time, are we?" he inquired acutely. "Figured on softening me up with a bit of cash, flooding my secrets out of me on a tide of gratitude?"

He shook his head. "Sorry. All my vices are literary these days, and even they aren't big or bad enough to make a fuss over. As my continuing absence from the review columns will attest."

He waved at his typewriter, which had a half-finished page stuck in it. "I was working when you arrived," he said, "and I'll be working after you leave. It's all I ever do, though I'm not sure why, any more. The definitive coming-of-age novel has been written. And Wes Bell wrote it."

"Kind of stole your thunder, didn't he? Your theme—what we give up when we grow up—it's the only thing you've ever cared to write about. You're a—"

"One-trick pony," he supplied. It was not the phrase I had been about to use, but it did the job.

"And yes," he allowed, "it galled me to see he could do it better than I. Disgusted me, in fact, although I find most books disgust me nowadays. If they're worse than mine I'm disgusted with them, and if they're better I'm disgusted with myself. But that's not the reason why I hated him."

He got up from his chair and shambled past me over to the bookshelves, pulled out a slender hardback volume. "*Harlan* wasn't his first book, you know. This one was."

He handed it to me and when I saw the letters on the spine I recognized it. *Webb's Lament,* a collection of Bell's early short stories recently issued in paperback on the strength of his great success with the novel.

I'd never seen the hardcover edition before, though, and it was a lovely job of bookmaking: acid-free paper, sewn signatures, figured end papers, all bound in soft forest-green leather. Just holding it in my hands made me wish that whoever invented perfect binding—the pernicious but economical process of simply gluing the pages into the spine of a book without first bothering to sew them into signatures, so the moment the book is opened the glue cracks and the pages at once begin falling out—had been smothered in his cradle with the same brisk heartless efficiency his work has given to the publishing industry.

Symonds stood over me. "Wes had this edition privately printed," he said, "only 750 copies. This one's number three. Open it, read the dedication."

I did, and it said: This book is for Reginald Nelson Symonds, my first and best teacher, with continuing gratitude and affection. Below in black ink was Wes Bell's strong back-slanted signature.

I looked at Symonds and caught the expression on his face before he turned away to hide it: grief and loss mingled with a kind of caustic unforgiveness that made me glad I was not the one who had betrayed him.

"So you were his mentor," I said, trying to make my voice light but knowing no amount of pleasantry could ever soothe or lighten this one. "Did you teach in high school, or something?"

When he turned back he was smiling, once more the cowardly lion or at least one who thinks the rage is no longer worth the roar. It made me wonder how many times he must have swallowed it, and how much it must have hurt him every time it went down.

"No. He wasn't that much younger, despite my mature appearance. We were friends. He wrote to me after my first book came out, *Father to the Man*. You remember that one?"

"Of course," I lied; I'd have told him I'd read *War and Peace* in the original Russian, if it might have made him feel better.

He smiled again, unfooled, and mercifully did not press me for plot details. "After that we wrote back and forth a lot. He was trying to get his first story bought and I suppose he thought I could help him. I was a big success in his eyes, then."

"And it did get bought," I prompted.

Symonds nodded. "In a horrid little rag, the kind of place that mixes up wretched and retched. Which was what I nearly did when I saw it, although naturally I didn't tell him so.

"Biggest thing that ever happened to him, and to celebrate he tossed a big bash at the country club his wife made him belong to—champagne, buffet supper and dancing, the whole nine yards. He even offered to pay for my plane ticket so I could show up, take my rightful share of the credit. So he said."

"How was it?"

Symonds shrugged. "Didn't go. My own wife was dying at the time, actually, a fact good old Wes never really seemed to absorb. It was as if, if it wasn't happening to him, it wasn't quite happening. If you see what I mean."

"I'm sorry about your wife. Then what happened?"

"Not much. Wes wrote more stories, sold 'em. I kept slogging away at the novel business. He wanted me to be his daughter's godfather, only his wife—"

"Corinna," I supplied.

"Yes, Corinna. What a sweet piece of poisoned fruit she turned out to be." Reggie had a nice touch for the descriptive phrase; too bad he couldn't write them as well as he pronounced them. The book Owen Strathmore had given me was well-conceived, professionally constructed and utterly, irredeemably boring.

"Anyway," he continued, "after that we lost touch. I think he was embarrassed about the way Corinna was toward me, and of course he got busier what with writing so much and teaching. I called him, though, right after I turned in my last book. He'd just gotten the Trout prize."

His mouth twisted bitterly. "I asked him for a blurb for my cover, begged him, actually. It would have made a difference, a few words from him on the front of my book. He said he was sorry but he never did blurbs. Didn't think his name should be turned into small change, he said, showing up on a lot of junk. Then he apologized, how thoughtless of him, he didn't mean my book was junk, of course. But I knew that was exactly what he did mean."

"And him an old friend who owed you one. Cruel of him."

"No. Not deliberately anyway, although I've heard he could be that too. Just...that was Wes. Eye on the main chance, devil take the hindmost."

I was beginning to find Reg's apartment remarkably comfortable and homelike. In the window he had set up a tiny bird-feeder where a cluster of finches squabbled amicably over a handful of seed. He was watching as he spoke and now a bluejay swooped down, driving off the smaller birds.

"I hated him, though," he added. "He made me see myself the way he saw me—a foolish old scribbler who doesn't even know enough to give up. And for that I don't think I'll ever forgive him. For that, I really could have killed him."

He glanced over, saw the look of pity on my face.

"Good at it, aren't you—getting people to tell you their little stories? Well, I'll tell you the rest of it, then. I saw him the morning he died. I knew he was coming to town for the workshop so I called him to ask him one more time to reconsider his decision. If my new book turns out yet another flop, I'll never get a contract to do more. I needed that damned blurb."

"Where did you see him?" I tried for a casual tone as I sipped at my cooling tea. He wasn't deceived, though. For once he had something to say that someone wanted to hear, and he was thoroughly enjoying the experience.

"Your office. The only place he would agree to meet me, where we wouldn't be seen together. Nice spot," he added, as apparently I did not look as if I believed him. "I like the new silver on the radiators. He was sitting behind your desk, by the windows."

He strode to his own window, shooed the jay with a violent wave of his big hand. "He knew what it meant to me, but he refused again. Told me to stop humiliating myself, he couldn't praise my book—it would discredit him in the industry to be linked with my sort of adolescent whining. So I hit him."

He smiled. "A solid right to the temple. God, it felt good. When I left he was rubbing his head and staring at me, as if he couldn't believe I had it in me. But," he added, "he was alive."

"You realize you're going to have to tell the police about all this. Or," I added, "I'll have to."

Reg looked unconcerned. "Yes, I guess I will, eventually. Or you can, I don't care. Just tell them what I've told you—that Bell was alive when I left him in your office."

"What if they don't believe that? The part about him being alive, I mean."

He came back to the coffee table, frowning at the remains of the snack he had laid out as if trying to remember what it was for.

"Then I suppose they'll arrest me, put me in jail. But that won't be so bad—once you get settled, I hear they let you have a typewriter, books, and so on. Hardly be much different from the way I live now, actually."

I thought Reggie's ideas about prison life owed a little too much to *The Bird Man of Alcatraz* and considered telling him this but he did not give me a chance to.

"And," he went on, "I'd get a bit of publicity out of it, too, wouldn't I? People might want to read a book by the fellow who killed Wes Bell—or by the one they thought killed him."

He plucked the money I'd given him from his pocket, dropped the bills on the table.

"Want this back? After all, if police are going to be here questioning me I won't have much free time to write any magazine articles."

I looked at the money, then at him again. The twinkle in his eye was not of good humor but of malice, pure and bitter as a drop of poison. I thought he could have killed Bell easily, and a man clever enough to survive all these years on what Reg earned might also be clever enough to pin such a crime on someone else. Someone like Owen Strathmore, maybe. He'd come up with the remark about my "playing detective" just a little too easily, as if he'd known it all along. And he did have the Geberth book.

On the other hand he hadn't had to tell me he'd seen Bell, or any of the rest of it, either. My instinct said he'd done it because he trusted me, maybe even wanted to help. And that, finally, was why I left the money where it lay.

"Until Friday," I told him as I headed for the door.

"Friday," he agreed distractedly, leaning down for the cash. When I looked back he was counting it again.

"Reggie." He stopped when he saw me watching. "How did you and Bell get into my office?"

Reg's shaggy brows went up. "He was there when I got there. I figured somebody else must have let him in."

"You didn't think that was kind of odd, without me around?"

For the first time he looked impatient. " 'There are many rooms in the mansion,' " he recited, "and most of them are governed by weirdness.' " Then he resumed counting twenties.

Hunter Thompson quotes, just what I needed to fill me with even more fear and loathing than two corpses already had. Now, though, an explanation for Bell's entry into my office occurred to me.

If he had not had a key, which I was pretty sure he hadn't, and Reg Symonds hadn't needed one—unless of course he was lying about Bell already being at my desk when he arrived—it seemed clear that the killer did have a key and had opened my office door before Bell got there, so that Bell would go in. That possibility was loathsome and fearful enough for me, making me wonder what other keys of mine a murderer might be running around with, and how fast I could get all the locks on Helen's house changed before someone surprised me some night with a visit.

All of these questions paled to utter unimportance, though, as making my way down the ill-lit staircase of Symonds's building I suddenly heard someone else following close behind me. Moments later a set of fingers roughly seized my wrist while another set clamped itself determinedly over my mouth.

SIX

"DON'T SCREAM. Please don't scream, I don't think I could take it if you—"

Having maneuvered me into a corner of the stairwell with both my arms twisted painfully behind me and my mouth full of his thoroughly unpleasant-tasting fingers, my attacker placed a knee very firmly in the small of my back. Meanwhile his thin boyish voice pleaded with me not to wound his sensibilities by yelling my head off about this the minute I got the chance.

Which was okay by me, since although he might not know it yet this guy's sensibilities were going to be the least of his problems the instant he let go of me. As far as I was concerned he could kiss his shrivelled gonads goodbye as soon as I got a finger free, and after that he'd better be wearing some serious eye protection or he could forget about reading any more comic books, too, in all the leisure time I was planning to create for him.

"Okay, now," he quavered. "Uh, listen, I'm going to take my hand off your mouth. I'm sorry about this, okay? I'm *really*—"

"You slimy sonofabitch, you let go of my hands right now or I'll—"

Ouch. His bony little knee bored into my sacroiliac. Oh, boy, was I ever going to hurt this guy, just as soon as I could move without fracturing important portions of my spinal column.

"Look," he begged, "be reasonable, I miscalculated, all right? I'm *sorry*. All I want to do is start over. Please."

"Grnl," I said.

"Okay, I'm letting go again. Everything's okay. Mistake, I just made small miscalcula—"

Turning, I reared back and socked him right between his beady eyes.

His body went flying, skinny arms flailing until he hit the bannister. Scrambling and grabbing he rescued himself from going over it, then sank to the stairs and bounced down three of them before stopping himself by clutching onto the balusters.

"Hey," he said, frowning up injuredly, "you didn't have to do that. I *said* I was sorry."

I reached down and grabbed him by his stupid string tie, and pulled up hard on it until his face was staring fearfully into mine. "You put your hands on me again, I'll bite them off. Do you understand? Because no one touches me until I tell them they can touch me. It's a little rule of mine, all right?"

I shook him, to punctuate this.

"All...all right," he gasped. "Uh, I can relate to that, sure. I mean I didn't mean any harm, I only wanted to—"

I slammed him against the balusters to get his attention. "People don't grab me, dimwit. People simply don't. I want an apology from you, and I want it right now."

"Right." His googly eyes rolled around in one of the most gratifying displays of abject terror I have ever witnessed.

"I apologize. I *sincerely* apologize. I will never ever again dare to touch you or approach you, or even look in your direction unless—"

"Shut up. Just shut up, and stand up. Walk down the stairs ahead of me, and if you meet anyone I hope you can summon up a smile because if you don't I'll reach down and snatch your kidneys out."

"Okay. Whatever you say." He clambered up, eyes fixed on my face.

"Good," I said. "You're doing very well." Then I followed him down the stairs and out the door, where of course he made a move to run for it as soon as he smelled fresh air. I quite naturally responded by tripping him, and he slammed like an underweight sack of horse manure to the sidewalk.

"What's this?" I asked, rummaging briskly in the inside pocket of his jacket and coming up with something hard and lumpy.

"It's just...it's just..." He made a snuffling sound.

"My goodness. Baby's got a weapon. I wonder what this was supposed to be used for?"

It was a tinny piece of junk, maybe forty-nine bucks in your local mayhem-and-macho supply emporium. Say what you want about handguns; personally I feel the only handgun that's safe is the one that's in my own hand.

"Walk," I said, prodding him with it, "to the corner where the red cop phone is hanging. When you get there stop, and other than that I strongly advise you not to move a goddamned inch."

"Uh-huh." He was weeping now, a scrawny little fellow with an unruly mop of brown hair, Coke-bottle-lensed hornrims, and a plastic pen-holder full of pens stuck in the pocket of his short-sleeved blue rayon shirt.

As I marched him down the street his arms and legs went every which way, not because he was trying to escape but because his peripheral nervous system was poorly linked to his central dispatching apparatus.

"Look," he babbled, "I'm a harmless guy, I only—"

"You only wanted what?" Cruelly I jabbed his little popgun in his ribs as I kept in step with him; ticked off as I was, he was lucky I didn't take his appendix out with it.

"To talk to you," he squealed. "I only wanted to—"

Without taking my eyes from him, I yanked open the emergency phone's red plastic cover. If there had happened to be a squad car around I wouldn't have had to bother, but you can never find a cop in the city when you want one; too bad, I thought, that I didn't happen to be dropping a candy-wrapper.

"I wanted to ask you what you'd found out about Wes Bell's murder," the squirming little goofball whimpered. "Because he said he would help me—I needed him to help me, and now he's dead. So how am I going to go on with my *career*, how can I do anything without the *advice* he was going to give me, the help and the *guidance* and all the tips on impressing all the *editors*, and—"

By then I had just about had it.

"Are you kidding? For that you ambushed me in a stairwell? What are you, nuts? What if *I'd* had a god-damned gun, for Christ's sake? You got a deathwish or what, binky?"

I shoved him against the phone pillar. "You attacked me," I told him. "You attacked me while concealing a deadly weapon. Which means you'd better have a lot better story lined up than the one you just tried sailing past me, fella, because I am not fooling around with you. You are going to be put in the custody of the police, and I am arranging that event immediately."

Whereupon he fainted.

If YOU WANT to think about a really frightening hazard to the public health, think about a general population that believes it knows how to do CPR but really doesn't. My attacker was lucky he survived the swarms of would-be paramedics flocking over his inert body like a bunch of mad scientists, eager to try out the techniques they'd only been able to practice in the lab so far.

"He's breathing, he's got a pulse!" I kept yelling as crew after crew of public-spirited pedestrians saw what they thought was going on and tried to straddle him. "He's only fainted!"

At last the squad car arrived. I told the officers what had happened and what I'd done, making sure they knew I was serious about everything I was saying since after all I did have the gun and the story did sound pretty ridiculous. On account of this I made sure I mentioned Mike Malley's name several times.

It didn't help, though, since believe it or not beat cops do not like finding angry women holding unconscious men at gunpoint on city streetcorners, and they do not like having civilians of any stripe using their private red telephones very much, either. Besides, like everyone else they only saw what they thought they saw—which did not particularly ease the pain of being booked at the Whalley Avenue Jail on one count of assault with a deadly weapon, one count of menacing with same, and one of calling in a false report.

"MR. WILLAMETTE," said the very stern lady public defender who at last came to talk with me, "has declined to press charges."

I kept my hands folded in my lap, as somehow I did not think it would be very politic to punch the lights out of the only person who could get me sprung from here. That pleasure would have to wait until I found Willamette, who if he knew what was good for him was getting his passport in order and choosing a foreign country to emigrate to right now.

Raising her lorgnette, the public defender peered at me.

"If," she said, "you agree not to harass him any further. Do you think you can promise that?"

"Oh, yes," I replied, "I certainly can promise that. I do promise it, in fact. Does that mean I can go now?"

For five-and-a-half hours I had been standing with seven other women in a holding cell designed to accommodate four. Three of the women were drunk and completely passed out, a circumstance for which I was grateful since it meant they did not talk at all. Three of the conscious ones were pros who wanted no truck with me and no trouble out of me, either, only that their pimps should get on down here and pay their bail pronto, so they could get back out to the businesslike operations of their franchises.

It was the other one I would have promised anything to get away from: a gum-cracking, shoulder-shrugging little sociopath in designer jeans, Frye boots, and a leather bomber jacket. Her name was Melissa and she had taught the bitch a lesson, all right, one she would be happy to repeat if the fat old hag ever tried pushing her around again. The fact that the fat hag in question happened to be her mother, whom she had allegedly stabbed twenty-seven times before setting their suburban house on fire, was as far as Melissa could see merely an unimportant side issue; the important thing was not having to hear any more unwarranted criticisms about her long-distance telephoning habits.

Strictly to avoid ever finding myself in the same room with her again, I cheerfully promised never to attempt entering any of the same rooms as Brady Willamette. Still, that didn't mean I couldn't catch him and make an example of him *outside* of any rooms, a thought which cheered me more than somewhat as I covertly went on entertaining it in action-packed full color stereophonic detail.

"Fine," said the public defender, not sounding particularly convinced but also not willing to make an issue of it; I got the idea Melissa was next on her agenda and she figured she'd better save her strength.

Personally I thought the only solution for Melissa was to send her back to the factory for some major wetware retooling. Luckily for her, however, I had not been put in charge of the system designed to stop these amok little shrapnel-bits of incomplete and inadequately organized human genetic material from violently impacting upon the lives of actual fully-formed normal persons. Instead, I was being released from the system.

And not in a very good mood, either, I'm sorry to report.

BRADY WILLAMETTE lived in a split-level ranch house about ten miles out of town, in a suburb so pretty I half-expected to see Dick and Jane romping with Spot on one of the green half-acre lawns.

As I arrived a grey-haired lady in a navy knit dress, beige support hose, and low-heeled navy pumps was coming out the front door, carrying a navy purse and white gloves in one hand, and a foil-wrapped pot of yellow chrysanthemums in the other.

"Oh, hello," she said. "I'm afraid if you're collecting for something or selling something I don't quite have time to—"

I opened her car door for her and she set her things inside, then turned back to me. "I'm on my way to my volunteer job, you see. Perhaps you could come back another—"

Her smile only faltered a little when I told her it was Brady I had come to see. "I've only just made his acquaintance," I explained, "but what he was telling me was fascinating and I'm afraid we didn't get a chance to finish our conversation."

"Really. Well then, why don't you go right on up and knock, dear. It's always lovely to meet any of Brady's friends."

As she spoke doubt and hope were warring on her pleasant face; Brady's friends probably didn't show up around here much unless someone happened to turn over rotted log. Behind her the curtain at the front window twitched and fell shut again.

"I'll just see if he's at home, then," I said.

"Oh, he's at home." With a last doubtful glance at me she got into the car. "He's... almost always at home."

Right, except when he was out playing with his toys. I gave her my most reassuring smile, just as if I hadn't come all the way out here for the specific purpose of smacking her son halfway into next week, and finally she drove away.

"Brady," I called, knocking hard. "Remember me, Brady? I'm the one getting ready to break this door down and drag you out by the hairs on your chinny-chin-chin."

"Go away! I don't want to talk to you. I said I was sorry and that's all I have to say!"

"Aw, that's too bad, Brady. Because I have something to say to you and if you don't let me say it I guess I'll have to wait right here until your mother comes home, and say it to her instead."

He opened the door at once.

"Come on, Brady, you wanted to talk to me before. Wouldn't you rather unburden yourself to me now than have good old Mom find out what a sneaky lying little slime-toad she raised?"

"She already knows that," he said sullenly, but he let me in and led me past the living room, through the kitchen toward a paneled stairway.

"After you," I told him, then followed him down into the finished basement where he apparently spent most of his time.

Ordinarily I might hesitate before doing any such thing, but I didn't think Brady was going to give me more problems now. Besides, if he did I could already tell which argument would work. I would just threaten to take away his bubble-gum for a week.

He was basically a big kid, and the basement he lived in was furnished with the kind of stuff a kid might inherit when his parents redecorate: a long horsehair sofa with a raggedy old knit afghan thrown across it, a battered recliner, random tables and lamps all stuck around any old way.

The items Brady had bought for himself were easy to pick out: an enormous color television hooked up to a cable box and a Nintendo controller. A computer with a modem and a list of about a dozen bulletin-board systems he could dial into when he got tired of playing by himself. A video cassette machine and a long shelf lined with old movies including the original *Blob*, Lon Chaney and Bela Lugosi hits, all the *Living Dead* films, plus a row of Three Stooges movies and Warner Brother's cartoons. No wonder he was so pale. The only light that ever hit his face came out of a cathode-ray tube.

"How did you get the police to believe your story?" I began, then turned around and stopped. Stuffed into built-in shelves that covered one whole wall of Brady Willamette's basement home was every book ever published on the topic of becoming a writer.

Books on how to write short stories, novels, jokes, song lyrics, poetry, screenplays, stage plays, and magazine fillers. The only thing missing was a book on how to write how-to books, an omission that made me want to call Bernie right now and see if he thought he could sell one of them because if there was one thing I sure as hell knew how to do it was write one.

The other thing Brady's books made me want to do, however, was sit down on the floor and weep. If he'd spent as much time writing as he seemed to have spent reading up on the topic of how to go about it, he could have been rich and famous by now, or at least not living in his mom's basement.

Or so I thought until Brady pressed one of his attempts into my reluctant hands.

"Here," he urged, "just read this. You'll see why I'm so darned upset. I know if I only could get a break . . . but no, *they* won't give it to me."

Writing, as the great Jacques Barzun has so beautifully pointed out, is not an enterprise in which one can succeed by the production of interesting fragments. Unfortunately for Brady Willamette, however, it is also not one in which the creation of ill-spelled, atrociously punctuated, grotesquely phrased and gratuitously violent claptrap is likely to get you very far, either, especially when it is printed out in the kind of pin-index typeface that resembles flat Braille.

The story, entitled "The Deadly Teenager," was about a boy who goes around murdering the prettiest and most popular girls in town, after they have shown by refusing to go out with him that they do not deserve to live.

Even this might actually have had some saleable potential had it been written in anything approaching standard English, and if in addition its author had not been quite so lip-smackingly on the side of the sadistic sophomore.

"Very impressive," I said, handing back the pages. "I can see you've put a lot of work into it. You were going to tell me how you got the police to believe you, though."

"I didn't have to get them to believe anything," he retorted loftily. "They know me. My father's an important politician."

He glanced protectively at the manuscript in his lap. "He doesn't live with my mother—she's just too boring and middle-class for a top guy like him to have to put up with. I'm always at the police station picking up details and story ideas, though, mostly at night when all the big important stuff is going down."

Uh-huh. Probably cheers and whistles from the boys in blue when they saw him coming, too. No wonder they were all in such a hurry to get rid of him.

"The gun," he told me patronizingly, "wasn't even loaded. You'd have seen that if you'd known how to check. And I have a carry-permit for it."

I smiled, filing the remark away for the future. Someday, I promised myself, I was going to take that gun away from him and beat him heavily about the face and head with it, and then tell him he had nothing to worry about because it wasn't even loaded and besides he had a permit for it.

"You were saying something about Wes Bell," I prompted him again. "Something about how he was helping you?"

Resentment clouded his face. "He promised. I went to one of those workshops—what a bunch of snobby bores there, treated me like I had herpes or something."

For a moment I almost sympathized with him, imagining the reception he'd gotten. To survive in that crowd, a buffoon like Willamette needed also to be some kind of idiot savant, a mathematical wizard or translator of Hebrew into Greek with a smattering of ancient Chinese and two or three obscure computer languages at his disposal. Otherwise they wouldn't even wait until he turned his back before they started snickering at him, which from his expression now I gathered they hadn't. But then his face brightened.

"Anyway, I got to talking with Wes. Man to man, you know, not that theoretical crap the rest of them were spouting. We hit it off right away, and when I said I was a writer too he invited me to his place."

I must have looked surprised. "In Manhattan?"

"Yeah. No big deal, just lunch and a couple of beers. Big apartment in the west eighties, you know. It's pretty nice, looks right out over the park. Wes showed me around, looked at some of my stuff, and

promised to introduce me to a couple of editors he
knew the next time I came down."

I thought about "The Deadly Teenager," which
bore about as much relationship to actual English
prose as a leaky bathtub bore to a floating sailboat,
and reflected that the only sort of refreshment Corinna Bell would be apt to offer Brady Willamette was
the kind you spray heavily around the baseboards of
your kitchen upon noticing unusual insect activity.

"Only now he's dead," Brady pouted, "so how can
he help me? I *need* some kind of—"

Right. Literarily speaking, Wes Bell was the hottest
ticket since Pete Rose and now he had croaked. No
more stories, no more novels, no more front-line report on the human condition by a guy who could make
that condition sing. For Bell, of course, the depriva-
tion was even worse: no more ice-cream sundaes, no
more sitting down with coffee and the newspapers, no
more hitting his trusty four-wood at the ninth hole,
birdying it easy with another nine left to play on a
sunny summer afternoon. No more anything for him,
in fact, and all it meant to Brady was that he couldn't
milk him for tips any more.

"Now wait a minute, Brady, let me make sure I've
got this straight. You showed your stories to Wes Bell,
and he said he was going to help you?"

Brady frowned stonily at me. "Oh, sure. You think
that's so unbelievable, don't you? You probably think
I'm just making it all up about getting invited and
having lunch with him and all."

He rummaged in a mess of papers in a heap by the
side of the recliner. "Well, ha-ha to you," he said tri-

umphantly, coming up with a well-thumbed sheet of pale blue stationery. "Here."

He thrust the paper at me, and it read: Dear Brady, Nice talking with you. Why don't you send me one or two more of your things—I'll see what I can do for you. Let me know next time you're going to be in town. Best—

The note was dated a month before and I recognized Bell's signature. Watching me read it, Brady Willamette puffed up with pride; I thought that with any luck at all maybe he would explode.

"See?" he demanded, grabbing his relic back and cradling it.

"Yes, Brady, I see," I told him, although what I really did see looked increasingly strange and unlikely.

Wes Bell—opportunistic poacher of other writers' ideas, victimizer and character assassinator of screwed-up young female critics, abandoner of his old friends and mentors, and if Owen Strathmore was to be believed a man who also beat up his wife—Wes Bell extending a helping hand to Brady Willamette? Sure, and right after that the members of the Junior League would be heading over in their pearls and their Perry Ellis leisurewear to some bombed-out tenements in the Hill Section of New Haven, set up a few coffee-klatches with the less fortunate of the drug-addicted welfare mothers in the neighborhood. Somehow there was something just a tiny bit out-of-focus about that scenario.

On the other hand, Brady did have the letter which on the face of it looked pretty legitimate: not only

Bell's signature but on his letterhead, and printed on his old Diablo 630 printer. I knew Bell's machine by the break in the serif of the 'y' on his pica daisy-wheel.

"You haven't," I said, "told me yet why this made you start following me. Or why you attacked me."

Brady looked pitying. "You still don't get it, do you? You still don't understand how bad it would have made them all look, how exposed they all would have been. Why, it would have ruined reputations, made fools of all the top people, shown them up for what they really are—"

"Brady. Slow down a minute. Who? Who would have been made fools of, and how?"

He smiled like a fellow who has long been in the know, and has at last been freed by circumstances to drop his confidential bombshell.

"Why, the people on the inside, of course. The ones who've been keeping me on the outside all this time—rejecting my work for their own stupid, selfish reasons."

His voice went up mimickingly. "'Sorry, Brady. Not good enough, Brady. Try again. Just not suited to our needs. Better luck next time, Brady.' And on and on when all the while the only reason was they just didn't want to."

He stomped around the basement room, waving the letter from Bell. "Their exclusive little club," he ranted, "oh *we've* all gotten published and *we* get to decide who else does, *we're* so important—"

He turned and aimed a finger at me. "Well, if they let in everybody who deserved it, then it wouldn't be so exclusive any more, would it? And they wouldn't be able to sneer and look down their noses while they ate their lunches in fancy restaurants."

He folded his arms. "But Wes," he went on, "was going to make them admit it. Once he started introducing me around they'd all have to start buying my stories, wouldn't they, and then what would they say about why they hadn't bought them before?"

I had to agree it made a kind of addled sense—the kind that is made by the sort of people who maintain lifetime memberships in the Flat Earth Society.

"Nothing, that's what," he answered himself. "They'd all be shown up as idiots, and they knew that, so they killed him."

He looked at me. "Someone killed Wes Bell to stop him from helping me," he said. "To keep me," he finished, "out."

Hoo, boy. For a moment I wasn't quite sure if that was the funniest story I'd ever heard, or the saddest. Then I glanced at Brady and knew it was the saddest. He was like the kid who never gets picked for the kick-ball team and can't understand that it's because he's wearing roller-skates.

I also thought that unless I appeared to give his tale my gravest and most serious consideration Brady's doors were going to come unhung from the couple of flimsy little hinges he still had holding him together.

"Anyway," he said, "I wanted to know what you were finding out, but I didn't want that Symonds guy to see and I thought he might look out his door, and then I got so nervous, and...I got a little carried away, I guess."

"I see." A little carried away—that was an interesting way of putting it. Maybe Brady had a future in political speech-writing. "How did you know I was trying to find out anything?"

"I told you," he replied impatiently, "I have ways of knowing stuff that's going on. Besides, he got killed in your office, didn't he? That much everyone knows, it was on the news. They called you a part-time writer and amateur sleuth."

In other words, he guessed and then he went off half-cocked. "Listen, Brady," I said, "we've got to make a deal, here. You can't be following me around, you'll get us both in trouble. I mean, look what happened today—that's not getting either one of us anywhere, is it?"

He looked at his shoes. "I guess not. But I'm not letting them get away with it, y'know. I'm gonna find 'em," he clenched his fists, "and then I'm gonna—"

"What if I were to give you a better idea?" I suggested, thinking that almost any idea would be better than the Byzantine schemes he was likely to hatch if left alone to it. Besides, he still had that cheap pop-gun in his possession. Probably the thing would blow up in his hand if he ever tried firing it, but by now I was feeling so sorry for the poor schmuck, I didn't even want that to happen to him.

"What idea?" He frowned suspiciously.

"I want you to write down everything you've told me today, and anything else you can remember. Get it down on paper, Brady. How you met Wes Bell, what he said, everything either one of you said when you went down to see him—all of it, you see?"

"Oh," he breathed. "I get it. Written proof."

"Well, not exactly proof." In the unlikely event that Brady thought this over later, I didn't want there to be too big a hole in the logic. Any gap bigger than a freight train he would probably see through pretty quickly.

"But a full account of all that went on," I told him, "will be useful, maybe even in court, and while you're writing it down you could remember something crucial. Who knows, this might be how you wind up nailing all your enemies—and the killer, too."

Now there was an idea that appealed to him. "Yeah. Okay, I think you've hit on something. Details, I've got to remember all the details. And how about all the arbitrary rejections I've had, and all the rudeness and people refusing to take my phone calls?"

"Put it all in," I said seriously. "Names, dates, times—go back through your mother's old telephone bills if you have to. Make it really complete. You never know what might be important."

There, that ought to keep him occupied for a while.

"But you'll keep me filled in, right, while I handle this end of things?" He followed me anxiously up the basement stairs. "If you find out any important facts you'll call me right away?"

I paused on the top step. "Brady," I assured him in my heartiest, most sincere voice, "if I come up with a single clue, I promise you'll be the absolute first to know about it."

Hey, so I lied.

"I KNOW HE'S HOPELESS, for heaven's sake—any fool can see he's hopeless. What I want to know is, is he dangerous? Has he got any priors, are people complaining about him, has he done any damage with that gun you jokers are letting him carry around in his goddamn jacket pocket?"

There was a brief silence on the other end of the telephone.

Then, "Charlotte," said Lieutenant Michael X. Malley, "it's been a long freakin' day."

"Yeah, right. Want to tip me off about whether or not I'm likely to end it up lying on a slab or not? I mean come on, Mike, is he a shooter or isn't he?"

The lieutenant let out a long, much-beleaguered sigh. "He is not a shooter. Far as I know, he is not even an aimer. If Brady Willamette could even figure out which end of a gun is the one you're supposed to point at a freakin' target I'd hand him a marksmanship medal myself, all right?"

All right. "So, what is he?"

"He's a flake," Malley replied tiredly. "He picked up a freakin' flake piece from his old man somehow—don't ask me how, and don't get me started on the old man, I'll pop a freakin' blood vessel just talkin' about him. Anyway, gimme a break, here, will you? It's late. I want to go home, for Christ's sake. Even a cop's gotta watch television sometime."

My turn to sigh. "Yeah, right. Okay. I don't know, though. This kid gives me a funny feeling."

Upon consideration the whole thing just didn't sit right with me, and it most certainly did not sit right with Solli who after hearing my report of the events of the day was getting ready to revoke my snooping privileges.

"He gives you a funny feeling," Mike Malley said irritably, "'cause you're a human and he ain't. It's like when a cat comes up against something that looks like a cat, and acts sorta like a cat, but it doesn't smell like a—"

"Okay, okay. He's on a short string, though, that's what you're telling me? Somebody supervises his activities?"

Malley made a noise. "If Brady Junior picks his nose, you can bet somebody's got the play-by-play. Hell, his old man's running for city council president next year, he's not gonna let some wacko little nebbish spoil his chances for that, even if it is his own son. Which he probably wishes he wasn't, but hell, that's life."

"So what is he, an axe-murderer?" Joey asked me breathlessly when I had hung up the phone.

If there is one guaranteed way to get your teenagers hanging wide-eyed upon your every word, it is to become involved even distantly in any activity that includes the wreaking of bloody mayhem. Just at the moment, though, I wasn't sure it was worth it. For one thing, it was too depressing.

"No," I said. "He's harmless. Just a little confused. Kind of sad and misdirected, that's all. He doesn't know what to do with himself, and he's got a whole lot of unrealistic ideas about wanting to do something he's not equipped to do."

"Oh," said Joey, disappointed. "You mean, like me thinking I'm going to be a pole-vaulter or an American League shortstop?"

"Yeah," I said, feeling a thump of pain at his words but not wanting him to see it. "Only Brady doesn't know he isn't, see? And he hasn't got anything else he wants to do instead."

I looked at Joey: brown hair, hazel eyes, the kind of grin that makes you think of Tom Sawyer. He really was just about the loveliest kid, and I'd have given my life to see him out of that chair—to see him walk just once on his own two feet again.

He knew, of course. "I guess," he said quietly, "this guy Brady just isn't as lucky as me, huh? I mean, nothing like a set of wheels to make a guy focus on his abilities."

He patted my arm. "Don't worry, Charlotte. It'll all be okay. Uh, listen, Myron's out front. He wants to know can he come in and apologize. He's awful sorry about last night."

I frowned. "Did his mother send him over?"

"Uh, no. Actually I called Mrs. Rosewater and asked her to let him come. She was pretty mad— madder than you, even."

The deliberate kindness of a sixteen-year-old boy is one of those remarkable energies which if it could be harnessed and distributed efficiently would put Con Edison out of business in about ten minutes.

Joey knew I missed Myron. There was just something about having a wiry black teenager constantly jitterbugging around my kitchen, singing all the words to all the hit songs in a high falsetto while predicting within two points where the Dow Jones average would end at the close of business tomorrow, that once I got used to it I simply could not seem to do without.

So I hugged Joey hard and then went out to the living room where Myron and Solli already were deep in a game of chess, and distracted Myron from his three-pawn attack on Solli's bishop by hugging him hard, too. After that of course I had to hug Solli, since he appeared to be feeling a little neglected, and finally we were one big happy family once more.

At least we were happy until Phileta Poole's evening nurse called to say that Phileta had slipped out again, she'd been gone for hours with no money and not even a sweater and no one knew where she was or what she might do; her emotional state was so terribly fragile lately and had I by any chance seen her?

Personally I did not think Phileta's emotional state was as fragile as all that, but of course I said I hadn't seen her and would keep an eye out for her. As I hung up the telephone it rang again. This time it was Anna calling to say that Owen hadn't been home all evening which of course worried her terribly as it just wasn't a bit like Mister Strathmore, so would I please, please try to find him? Because if not, she just did not know what she would do.

Naturally I said I would phone whoever I could think of, since the thought of Owen wandering around on his own at night was much more alarming even than the idea of Phileta wandering around on hers. Owen's idea of a wild evening was to have the radio playing while he read galley proofs of his latest *Exsanguinator* novel.

I hung up; the instrument began once more to shrill.

"Don't answer it," said Solli.

"I'll get it," offered Joey, "and I'll tell 'em you've gone to Timbuctoo."

Disregarding these suggestions I decided reluctantly that I might as well answer it myself. Considering the way the calls had been going so far I thought that whatever it was now could hardly be any worse.

In this however I turned out to be mistaken, as when I did at last pick up the phone it was the typist calling to say she was pretty sure Reggie Symonds wouldn't be delivering those two *Pen and Pencil* articles he had promised by Friday, since someone had just murdered him.

SEVEN

"WHAT DO YOU MEAN," I asked Mike Malley incredulously, "where do I think he would go? How do I know where Owen Strathmore might go—he's never gone anywhere before."

Lieutenant Malley stood over the sprawled form of Reggie Symonds, eyeing the corpse with distaste while chewing the unlit stub of his horrid cigar and not bothering to remove his pork-pie hat in the presence of the deceased.

His fat fingers clenched and unclenched, his thick neck creasing as he glared up at me. From the floor by his feet Reggie Symonds glared too, only not at anything.

"Yeah, well, we got a witness saw him here," Malley growled, "so put your thinkin' cap on." He winced, and put a hand to his belly. "Guy's screwin' up my freakin' digestion."

"Witnesses?" I looked around. "What witnesses?"

Reggie's apartment appeared pretty much as I had seen it earlier, except that all the crackers and cheese were gone, along with most of the grapes. On his door-and-sawhorse desk were an open spiral notebook and six freshly sharpened pencils, one of them still lying across a page of the notebook.

He'd been working on my articles, I realized, recognizing the compulsive habits of a careful first-draft writer. Someone had knocked on his door, he'd frowned at the interruption and laid down the pencil to go see who it was, and...

"Neighbor lady," Malley scowled, "heard a commotion."

He massaged his belly again. "Goddam cruller I ate, musta been stale. You gotta 'nough pictures, you guys?" he asked the technicians working around him.

The technicians were taking polaroids and dusting surfaces with their small soft brushes, picking up bits of matter in tiny tweezers and dropping the bits into labeled plastic bags.

"Better hurry up," he advised them, "'fore the chalk fairy gets here. No matter how many times you tell 'em," he grumbled to me, "first thing somebody always wants to freakin' do, draw a goddamn line around the dead guy. Like he's maybe gonna freakin' escape or something, they don't fence him in fast enough."

"What neighbor lady?" I persisted. "She said she saw Owen? How did she know it was him?"

I stood in the hall on the other side of the two-inch-wide yellow plastic tape stretched across Reggie Symonds's doorway. The black letters on the tape read NHPD DO NOT CROSS THIS LINE NHPD.

"Six feet plus inches tall, maybe three hundred pounds, red shirt, blue coveralls, red suspenders," Malley replied. "Bald as a billiard ball. That sound familiar to you?"

I sighed. Owen Strathmore was pretty hard to miss.

"Also," Malley said, "he was holding a gun. He pointed it at the neighbor lady, she sticks her head in to see what's goin' on. She screams, runs back an' calls the cops while he departs.

"So what I wanna know is," Malley jabbed the cigar stub my way, "where does a three-hundred-pound bald guy hide, nobody is going to notice he's suddenly showed up there?

"Or," he added significantly, "maybe they do but they're not going to say anything about it, like maybe they're on his side."

"Not me," I protested stoutly. Reggie continued glaring fixedly at nothing, as if being found dead this way merely added insult to injury; why, he seemed to wonder, could he not have attracted this much attention when he was alive?

"Yeah, yeah." Malley sounded unconvinced, his fingers still prodding uneasily at the area above his belt buckle.

"Hey, lieutenant, this guy's got a lot of money on him. It looks like about three hundred bucks, here."

"That's mine," I said, stepping forward, and the dark-suited man probing delicately in Reggie's pocket looked up at me. Mike Malley looked at me, too, eyes narrowing with renewed interest.

"I paid him for two pieces of writing," I explained, "and since he's obviously now not going to supply them—"

Malley made a face. "List it and get it in a valuables envelope," he ordered the technician. "Anybody wants anything out of this guy, they can freakin' petition his estate."

Hey, it was worth a try.

"You got any idea why somebody'd want him dead?" Malley demanded. "Anybody got a beef with him, you know of?"

I shook my head. "I've only met him twice, but as far as I could tell he wasn't important enough to hate. Not this much, anyway."

"Okay, lieutenant, we're done," said one of the technicians, and at the words a very young uniformed officer with a big piece of chalk in his hand stepped forward alertly.

Crouching, the officer began to draw a thick chalk line on the floor around Reggie Symonds's corpse. When he had finished and the medical guys took Reggie away, what remained was a rough cartoon of a man with one arm thrust up as if trying to stop traffic or hail a cab. Dusting the chalk powder from his hands, the young officer looked pleased with himself.

"Ain't that the way of it," Malley said in disgust. "Guy's a nobody, somebody blows him away an' I gotta get gas pains out of it. Story of my freakin' life."

He eyed me with continued suspicion. "How'd you find out about this so fast, anyway? You're getting to be like flies, all the time showin' up soon as somethin' starts to stink."

I didn't think it would be a good idea to bring the typist into this, especially since the way she found out was via a friend of hers who happened also to be a cop. It seemed she was sitting with him in his squad car in a secluded location, which was probably enough to get him busted to foot patrol, and heard the whole thing over his radio, including the identity of the deceased.

Luckily, just then a particularly vicious pang of indigestion seized Malley's whole attention.

"Oof," he said, looking even greyer and unhealthier than usual, which for Malley was saying quite a lot. Little beads of sweat popped out below the brim of his hat. Grimacing, he mopped them with a handkerchief.

"Lieutenant," I said, "are you sure you're all—"

"G'wan." He pressed his fist into his solar plexus. "I'm fine. I could get away from all the ding-dongs shootin' holes into other ding-dongs once in a while, I'd be Mister freakin' Universe."

He pulled a roll of Tums from his rumpled jacket pocket and popped a handful of the tablets into his mouth, crunching them in his teeth with a sound like small stones being pulverized.

"Tell you something, though," he said through a mouthful of the dissolving antacid medicine, "you hear anything outta that"—he swallowed shudderingly—"that freakin' Strathmore, you get on the horn to me. I don't mean ten minutes later, I mean like right now. You get a call from him, I get a call from you, got it?"

"Got it," I said, feeling suddenly confident about making this promise since it had just occurred to me where Owen almost surely was headed, and if I was right I would not be getting any calls from him because they did not have any telephones there.

"RED ALERT," I told Joey early the next morning. "Battle stations. That means you do absolutely nothing unless you are absolutely sure I would say okay about it if I were here. If you aren't sure you don't do it, are we clear on that?"

"Yes, ma'am," Joey responded in the serious, adult tone of voice he always uses when he is getting ready to cross his eyes and stick his tongue out at me as soon as I turn my back.

I rounded abruptly on him; the tip of his tongue vanished back into his mouth.

"Charlotte," he said, "you're only going for one night. I'm not a little kid, you know."

In my mind, of course, that was exactly what he was. But if I said so he would only want to prove otherwise, and as this was what I was hoping to avoid I studiously ignored his comment.

"Here's a list of phone numbers you can call if you have any trouble, or if you need anything. There's sandwich material in the refrigerator and milk in the jug, and—"

"I know, I know, a casserole thawing out on the counter. I can see it." His face expressed what he thought about it, too.

"But," he made his eyes ridiculously huge and woebegone, "who's going to tuck me in and read me a bedtime story, and kiss me goodnight?"

I slugged him gently on the jawbone, then planted a big smacking kiss on the same spot. "There, that ought to hold you."

He squirmed away in mock disgust. "Yechh, people lips."

"—and we'll be home tomorrow evening," I finished, "so please don't go out because if I get here and you're not here you know I'll probably have a nervous breakdown."

His face changed, becoming all at once the face of the grown man he would be in only a few more years. "Yeah, okay. You know, you worry about me too much, Charlotte."

I paused in my whirl from icebox to breadbox to the cache of milk money, lunch money, hacking-around money, and emergency money I had hidden away for him in the corner of the silverware drawer.

"I know," I said. "I know I do." Just then Solli came in to report that the bags were loaded, the route was all plotted out and the map was marked, and did I think I would be ready soon or should we just let the car sit there running in front of the house until it was out of gas and we could forget the whole thing?

I ran quickly once more through my mental list, discovering that everything on it had been checked off including the two envelopes propped up on the kitchen table, one clearly labeled "paperboy" and the other clearly labeled "typist," since while the paperboy probably would enjoy finding a check for $274.97 in his envelope I did not think the typist would at all appreciate finding bills and change totalling $4.75 in hers.

"Charlotte," said Joey in the gently pitying tone he always uses when I really am being silly, and not just careful.

"Charlotte," said Solli in the businesslike tone he always uses to indicate that if I do not hurry up he is going to go out there right now and take all the bags back out of the car and leave them on the sidewalk for me to bring in myself, dammit.

"All right," I said, hugging Joey and holding him away from me one more time, foolishly certain all at once that I would never, ever see him again. Then, squaring my shoulders and stiffening my lip, I strode out to the car. Solli had already aimed it in the general direction of the White Mountains of New Hampshire, since this was where I meant to find Owen Strathmore and make him tell me what the hell he had been doing standing over poor old Reggie Symonds's body with murder in his eye and a gun in his hand.

FROM A DISTANCE, the Mount Washington Hotel resembles the wedding-cake of a mad Bavarian prince: an enormous many-turreted structure of white frosting trimmed with mint-green spun sugar, topped by a final tier of red sugar glaze and decorated in dozens of tiny, smartly-snapping banners. It's only from a distance that the hotel can be seen entirely, as once one begins to make one's way up the long road toward it its hugeness closes in so that one can only see part of it: a long white veranda curving whitely away like an artist's exercise in perspective. Roses and zinnias, tulips and hyacinths, masses of geraniums and thousands upon thousands of daffodils landscaped into sloping flower-gardens. Box-hedges trimmed into topiary animals, fountains spraying fist-sized gouts of water at an unbelievably clear blue mountain sky, groupings of white wicker armchairs with sea-green linen cushions, the occupants of which are accepting refreshments from frilly-aproned waitresses.

At the head of the formal entrance-drive, beyond the row of Lincoln town cars and BMW sedans and Mercedes coupes all waiting to be put away by an efficient-looking tag-team of valet parking attendants, a silver-haired gentleman in grey flannel slacks and blue blazer offers to deal with one's car and one's baggage, and to shuttle one's golf clubs conveniently off to the pro shop, too, if that is what one desires.

And at the Mount Washington, of course, that is what one desires, for at the Mount Washington there is nothing to do but be catered to in every way imaginable.

This however did not go down well with Solli, who does not like having other people carrying his bags or his golf clubs or messing about with his car; he feels it is undemocratic.

"Let the people earn their living, for heaven's sake," I told him, "how can they possibly make any decent tips if do-it-yourselfers like you go on nobly refusing their services?"

Then I nudged him gently but firmly in the direction of the bell-captain, who seemed quite bemused at the sight of a man with three suitcases, a carry-all, and a beat-up-looking cloth bag of mismatched golf-clubs staggering determinedly at him across the crystal-chandeliered and Aubusson-carpeted Mount Washington Hotel lobby.

"I'll take care of that, sir," the bell-captain said as he unburdened Solli in a twinkling. Moments later the bags had vanished out of sight as if by magic, and Solli was blinking the way he does when a new idea has just struck him.

"Strathmore," I said to the brisk young woman at the front desk, having just sold my credit-card into indentured servitude forever for the privilege of spending a night here.

"We're not really certain," I went on, "but if he did decide to come up we are hoping to join him for cocktails."

Behind me I could feel Solli frowning, since cocktails are yet another civilized custom of which he does not fully approve—chiefly because he has not learned to drink one of them without falling down afterwards.

"No, I'm afraid he's not registered," said the young woman. "Would you like to leave a message, in case he does come in?"

I declined; if Owen was here under a false name it would be useless, and if he came in later and registered under his own name it might frighten him away, and then I would never find him.

As it turned out, though, I needn't have worried about that. From behind me sounded a voice like a familiar foghorn:

"Charlotte," Owen Strathmore said, "I'm over here."

"No television," observed Solli disapprovingly when we had been conducted to our tiny room, with Owen following anxiously along behind us like an abnormally large and insecure five-year-old.

"Also," Solli said, his frown deepening as he took in the scarcity of dresser drawers and reading lamps and the extreme elderliness of woodwork, wallpaper, and plumbing fixtures, "also no radio and no refrigerator."

The room, which had obviously once been a servant's room connected to the larger suite directly adjacent, smelt faintly of age and mothballs. Pipes crisscrossed its ceiling, two long deep depressions marked the ancientness of the double bed, and the transom over the hall door had been painted shut. Edging between the bed and the room's only decent chair, I reached the window and snapped the yellowed shade up, at which Solli brightened at once.

From the hotel's back lawn a short sharp slope downward led to swimming pools, tennis courts, horse-shoe pits, bridle paths, putting greens, a fly-fishing stream, and an eighteen-hole championship golf course with which the green valley stretching away to the mountains had thoughtfully been furnished.

"Camp," said Solli in tones of delighted discovery, "that's what this place is. A summer camp for grown-ups."

So he changed into his play clothes and went cheerfully off to investigate his chances of making up a foursome before dinner, as he thought there must still be time to get in at least nine holes and possibly even eighteen if they decided to take a cart.

Meanwhile I guided Owen to the hotel bar. While Solli indulged himself in a little healthful exercise I meant to indulge myself in a good stiff belt of Scotch, and preferably in more than one.

"Here," I said, handing Owen his drink and settling him in a chair on the veranda. From here we could gaze out over the valley to the mountains beyond while around us laughter from the tennis courts mingled with the twittering of swallows swooping overhead, and with the tinkling of silverware and clinking of china as the hotel dining room geared itself up for dinner.

It was a perfect place for sharing secrets, and I planned to pry all of Owen's out of him before getting him so drunk he would barely be able to walk, much less run. Then I would sit him down to an enormous dinner and roll him immediately to his bed, where for a few hours at least I would not have to worry about him.

Unfortunately the line between Owen drunk enough to talk and Owen sober enough to talk was vanishingly slender, and in order to negotiate it I was forced to imbibe somewhat myself.

"Just put them down there," I told the waitress carefully as she arrived with our third round of double Scotch sours.

Then I turned back to Owen. "All right. You were worried, you didn't have anybody to talk to, and you didn't want to bother me. That much I understand," I said, ignoring the really quite startling unlikelihood of this as in my experience people actually prefer to bother me, and will in fact abandon a number of much more attractive activities in order to do so.

"But why call Reggie?" I pressed. "I thought you thought he was contemptible."

"He *was* contemptible," Owen said, "as a writer. And of course, when he was still alive. But now that he's dead . . ."

His lower lip quivered; I thrust the new Scotch sour hastily at him.

"He was like me at heart," Owen went on after he had sucked at it. "Foolish old hack, getting thick around the middle while his books and papers piled up around him and his chances thinned out. And I just thought..."

"You thought Reggie would understand," I suggested, and Owen nodded energetically.

"Yes," Owen said, "and you know, he really seemed to. He said I ought to come over, just come on right now and not bother about what he had been doing. Said he'd take care of it later."

Poor old Reggie, what a gentleman at heart. "And so you did go over. How? In your car?"

Owen shook his head. "No. It's only twenty blocks or so, you know, and on such a night—well. I was afraid, Charlotte. I was afraid that soon I might be locked away forever. I didn't want to miss the last spring evening I might ever have."

He looked down at his lap. "Only when I got there, he was dead. I knocked on his apartment door—the lower door, the one to the street, had been propped open—and when I did it swung inward. And...and I saw him lying there."

Owen stopped, huge shoulders trembling, his eyes bright with the memory of sudden shock.

"I've wasted so much of it, Charlotte," he said quietly when he spoke again. "Time, spring evenings, people—I've made such a balls-up mess of it."

Uh-oh. If I let him dissolve in tears now, he'd float away on a tide of booze and self-pity, and then I'd never get any more answers out of him. Not, at least, until it might be too late.

"Owen, thousands and thousands of people enjoy your books. Maybe even millions—they're all your friends, you know, even if they haven't ever met you."

Probably because they hadn't, as a matter of fact, but this was not the right time to say so. "Buck up, now, and tell me all about what happened after you found Reggie."

Owen sniffled, drew out a huge red handkerchief, and favored it with an enormous honking blow. From wicker chairs all up and down the veranda smooth heads turned and well-shaped eyebrows lifted in civilized affront.

I smiled apologetically, mentally giving all these well-bred types a liberal dose of my middle finger; god forbid any of them should have to witness anything resembling a legitimate emotion being expressed, since most likely they had not thought to pack along the costume for it.

"You found him," I prodded Owen, "and then what did you do?"

"Then," he said, "I hurried in. I bent down beside him and saw he must be dead, or at least awfully close to it, and thought I've got to call for help for him, I didn't have any idea what to do. So I looked for the telephone, and that was when I heard the sound."

A sound, I thought, feeling pleased: how interesting, and in addition how utterly congruent with my developing theory.

"What sort of sound?" I queried gently, not wanting to bump Owen's train of thought off its shaky track.

"Laughter," he replied, "evil-sounding laughter—and then footsteps coming nearer. The gun lay by his head. I grabbed it, sure that in a moment I would confront his killer. Then—"

"Then?" I urged him delicately, but when I looked at him I realized Owen had passed out.

"You know," I told Solli several hours later, "if men start going unconscious on me like this all the time I'm just going to have to shoot myself. First Willamette and now Owen."

Solli considered this for a moment. "Yeah," he said. "I don't blame you. What a drag. Poor Owen too, though," he added.

Having stowed Owen fully-clothed in his bunk, we had eaten dinner in the dining room—an experience which was, by the way, one of the most frustrating exercises in the postponement of gratification I have ever endured. The food itself was wonderful; awaiting the attentions of someone who could put some of it onto one's plate, however, required a kind of Zen-like discipline.

Afterwards we'd driven to a small general store where they sold newspapers, Fig Newtons, and bottles of fruit juice, which we took back to our room for a late-evening picnic.

"It's perfectly obvious what happened," I said, munching. "Whoever killed Symonds was still there when Owen arrived, and couldn't resist gloating. Watching while Owen found the body and even laughing—what a cold heart that took. Owen was probably right to grab the gun—I think I'd have grabbed it, too."

"Where, though?" Solli objected. "Where was the killer, I mean? Inside the apartment?"

I nodded, chewing on a Fig Newton. "Must have been. The neighbor lady would have seen, otherwise. What I want to know is, why kill Reggie Symonds?"

"To stop him from telling you something?" Solli suggested.

I shook my head. "Doesn't make sense. In the first place, I don't think Reggie knew anything except that Wes Bell was a rat, which everyone but Brady Willamette seems to have known. He practically worshipped Bell, and still does."

I swallowed some fruit juice. It made a nice change from Scotch sours, which I didn't think I would ever be able to look at again. "Besides, if someone thought Reggie knew something incriminating, why wait? The sensible time to kill him would have been much earlier, right after killing Bell. As it is, someone dawdled until after I'd—oh."

Solli put down his newspaper. The look on his face said he was thinking the same thing I was. "Maybe," he said slowly, "it wasn't about Reggie telling you something. Maybe somebody thought you'd told him something, and somebody didn't want him to tell anybody else."

"Oh, dear. Then I doomed him by going up there, didn't I?"

But Solli was shaking his head. "No, wait a minute—that doesn't make any sense either. Because if it's something you know that the killer wants kept quiet, why not just . . ."

He stopped, but unfortunately my thought processes didn't.

"Right," I said. "I'm the one who found Bell. Perhaps when I did that, I also found something else—something even I don't realize I found."

That was it, I felt sure. It even explained the falling concrete block. Whatever the deep dark secret was, I apparently knew it. I just didn't know I knew it. Somewhere out there, though, was somebody who did.

"So why has the killer not tried again to kill me? Yet," I added bleakly.

As it turned out, I was wrong about the Mount Washington Hotel not having any telephones. Wishful thinking on my part, I suppose, as the idea of a place without any of these troublesome instruments is to my mind right up there alongside those two other examples of unreachable perfection, the prompt, accurate bi-annual publisher's royalty statement and the all-you-can-eat cold lobster buffet, neither of which I expect actually to see in my lifetime and especially that royalty statement.

Not only did the Mount Washington have telephones, in fact, but my very own room was equipped with one, and it was ringing when I woke up the following morning.

"Mmph," I said, and Bernie Holloway's voice came on.

"Listen, Charlotte, you know I have the deepest concern for your health and all that, but isn't this a kind of funny time to be taking a vacation? I mean, Phil Poole's guy just called and he wants to talk to you about the anthology, and he also wants to know if they'll be getting *Pen and Pencil* layouts on time, and not only that but from the way the guy was pressing me I think Poole also thinks you've got his daughter hidden away somewhere, ha-ha, although I put the kibosh on the idea toot-sweet."

He paused to draw breath. "I was right about that, wasn't I, Charlotte? I mean, you're not up there playing amateur shrink to the little crackpot, are you?"

At that moment Owen Strathmore came shambling in, admitted by Solli whose brain had apparently gone momentarily even softer than his heart. No, I wanted to say. I'm up here playing amateur shrink to a great big crackpot.

"She's not as crazy as you think, Bernie. In fact, she's really not at all—"

"Oh, god," said Owen, putting his hands cautiously to his head. "Coffee, I want to drown in an ocean of coffee."

"What was that?" Bernie asked, alarmed. "It sounds as if you've got a moose in the room with you."

"Never mind," I said hastily, then covered the phone with my hand and shooed both men downstairs with orders to find several enormous pots of hot coffee and bring them back here immediately, as the day I leave a hotel room without having first had at least two cups of coffee is the day I will be carried dead out of it.

"How," I demanded of Bernie when they had gone, "did you find out I was here?"

"Joey told me. Look, Charlotte, Poole's really getting whacked out about his daughter being gone and somehow he's got the idea you're involved. He's talking about sending private detectives out looking for you, for god's sake."

Yeeks. Considering how Phileta had last fared with those fellows, I'd as soon have had a team of hired assassins chasing after me.

Come to think of it, I probably already had one assassin chasing after me, although whether hired or not I could not yet be sure, and meanwhile Joey was busily informing all and sundry of my current whereabouts.

"Bernie, you didn't tell Poole where I am, did you?"

"No, but—you don't have her, do you, Charlotte? Because if you do I hate to say it but you have blown off nine-tenths of your income for this year. Poole is never going to let you finish that anthology if you've got her, and I've given away all the scut-work I can find to a woman in Burbank who thinks she's the next Mary Higgins Clark, although I'm sorry to report that from what I've seen out of her so far she is mistaken."

Right. Thanks, Bernie, for reminding me just which rung I occupy on the ladder of literary accomplishment. So heartening, these little pep talks.

"I don't have Phileta, Bernie. I don't know where she is, and I certainly do not hope to find her, either, since for all I know she could very well have killed Wes Bell and Reggie Symonds, or gotten someone else to kill them for her."

"Good heavens," said Bernie.

"And," I went on, "if she did then I very much fear that on her list of enemies my own name has begun to figure prominently."

After all, I knew she had been loose when Bell and Symonds died. "Anyway, tell Poole I'm putting him together a table of contents for the book, the layout sheets for *Pen and Pencil* are being pasted up now, and I sincerely hope he finds Phileta. Honest, Bernie, I'd tell you if she were here."

"All right," Bernie said doubtfully, not believing a word of this which was actually pretty smart of him since hardly a word of it was true. "I'll talk to you later, then."

"Fine," I agreed, hanging up and pulling on my robe to go and answer a knock on the door, this being my second mistake of the day right after answering the telephone.

"Well, it certainly took you long enough," I began crossly.

Then I stopped. Just outside the door, Solli stood holding a tray loaded down by five pots of coffee and five cups, and as there were only three of us this alerted me at once.

Why, oh why, I asked myself, did I ever have to teach Joey to be so polite and helpful on the telephone? Why couldn't I have taught him to demand a secret password and then hang up rudely on anyone who didn't know it?

Because that was what had happened, of course. People had asked Joey where I was and he had told them. Slowly I looked up, not wanting to see what I knew I must see. Or rather, whom.

"I couldn't just leave them down there in the lobby, could I?" Solli said, making an I-can't-help-it face as he led them in.

"Sorry, Charlotte," Owen mumbled, edging past me in hang-dog fashion.

"Hi," David Fischer ventured uncertainly, coming in behind Owen.

That left one person still standing out in the corridor, looking just about as murderous—and about as much in control of her own destiny—as an infant abandoned in a basket on the front steps of the orphanage.

"Hello, Charlotte," whispered Phileta Poole.

"I GOT SCARED," David Fischer explained simply. "Reg Symonds hated Wes Bell, and now he's dead. Phileta hated him—"

At the sound of her name, Phileta Poole shrank even more into herself. She would not take coffee or even sit down on the bed, preferring to stand by the window as if contemplating whether or not to jump out of it.

"—and she showed up on my doorstep like this, all freaked out." Fischer went on.

"I was scared, too," Phileta said, stepping in. "I'd met David a long time ago at a college writing conference, and when I couldn't find you I remembered he lived in New Haven, too."

"You," Fischer pointed at Owen, "are now being hunted on suspicion of two murders on account of having—or not having, I'm not sure which—an affair with the guy's wife. Which is ridiculous. Everybody knows you don't do anything but write."

Owen bristled faintly at this, then sank back into miserable immobility.

"And you," Fischer pointed at me, "are hooked up in it too, which I also can't understand, but at least you had the brains to get out of town and considering what's happening to other people who hated Bell the way I hated him, I figured that was a great idea. So," he finished, "we followed you here."

He really was good-looking in an over-intense sort of way—dark hair, dark brooding eyes, long flight fingers—and for a moment I considered trying to pair him off with Phileta. This of course would not even have begun to solve any of their problems; still, human physiology being what it is I thought it might take the edge off for a while, and besides here we all were already conveniently installed in a hotel.

Unfortunately, however, David Fischer did not seem to have brought his blowtorch along, and this was what it would have taken to unfreeze Miss Poole.

"Oh," she whispered strickenly, staring out the window at the mountains. They did not appear at all murderous from here, but that did not change the fact that every year several people died upon them simply through having mistaken their essential nature: unpredictable, uncaring, utterly and entirely merciless.

But for me and thee, I thought silently at Solli, and his answering look agreed with me. Up until now I had also exempted Owen from any thought of suspicion, but I couldn't anymore; like the mountains, all my visitors just looked too innocent.

If David Fischer had killed Bell and Symonds and the poet—the first out of hate, the other two to try covering his crime somehow—then it was to his advantage to seem frightened.

And if Phileta had done it she was wise to seem bizarre: fully, harmlessly, and naturally. Unfortunately for her, though, I'd already seen her when she wasn't. However upset she might be now, she was no more nuts than I was; of that I was quite sure.

If Owen had done it, though, then he was the smartest one of all: help me, Charlotte, I haven't an idea what to do next.

Of course if he did know what to do he was doing it in spades. The thought gave me some pause as I had never sat in a room full of murder suspects before, and on top of the ones already present there were still Brady Willamette and Corinna Bell to be reckoned with, their unpleasant images jumping suddenly and vividly to mind as a second knock came—slowly, deliberately, ominously—upon the door of my room at the Mount Washington Hotel.

"Message for you, ma'am," said the bellboy, handing over an envelope and accepting the dollar bill I thrust at him. The others looked on interestedly as from the envelope I drew out a single sheet of hotel notepaper and read it.

"Well," I said, smiling with all the pleasant insincerity I could muster, "isn't that nice." I handed the note to Solli.

"What is it?" David Fischer asked as, taking my cue, Solli also managed to look pleased.

"Nothing to do with you," I assured him, "or with any of you," I added, frowning at Solli to make him stop pursing his lips. "I seem to be getting a mention in the *Times* today, and my editor wants to make sure I see it, is all."

Much more of this and my nose was going to start growing.

"Now *you*," I told Phileta, "are going to go in there and take a hot shower, and afterwards I will lend you something clean to put on."

I turned to Fischer. "And *you*," I said, "are going to take Owen downstairs and make him eat breakfast, and from the looks of you I think you'd better eat some, too."

Phileta blinked and began numbly following instructions. Owen, raising his bulk from the room's only decent chair, lumbered out after David Fischer and the hallway door closed behind them.

Hearing the shower hiss on I turned to the phone, but Solli was already dialing it.

"No answer," he said. "Maybe he went out and forgot to turn on the machine."

"Only," I said, "for that to be true he'd have had to turn it off first, because I'm really pretty sure I left it set."

"Or," Solli said, "there could have been a power outage, and you know when that happens it erases the outgoing message and the machine doesn't—"

"Oh, I hope not. Poor Joey—all alone without any lights, not even any way of fixing himself anything hot to eat—"

"Charlotte, I don't think the temperature of Joey's evening meal is exactly the crux of the matter here, do you?"

Frowning, he dialed our home telephone number again with the same unsatisfactory result. Then we tried the Rosewaters and the typist and everyone else we could think of, but none of them were answering either.

"Okay, that's it," he said. "You pack the stuff, I'll get the car. See if you can shout some muscle tone into Phileta before she slips down the shower drain, and if you can find a bellboy with a whip and a chair have him round up those other two dimwits, too."

This for Solli was very strong language indeed, but then he was provoked. Thrusting the note at me he slammed irritably out.

I was provoked, too, and now that I could not raise Joey I was also very frightened. Sitting on the bed I read the message again, hoping to find it somehow less worrisome than before.

But it wasn't.

EIGHT

"I DON'T GET IT," Joey said a little defensively. "I've been home all the time and I answered the phone when it rang, so what exactly is the problem, here?"

I looked at Joey, at the answering machine which was turned on and correctly set, and then at Joey again.

"You're sure," I said, "you didn't go out."

At this he looked insulted. "You know, Charlotte," he said, "if I were a liar, I wouldn't be a stupid liar. If I had gone out and didn't want you to know, I'd have definitely left the machine on and said I was asleep or had my headphones on, or something. And anyway, I'm not a—"

"Of course you're not," I apologized immediately, turning to Solli. "Someone seems to be having a little fun, making me think he—or she—can get in here any time, and do whatever—"

"Never mind making you think it," Solli said. "Somebody did." He got up from where he had been examining the telephone jack.

"Two nights ago," he explained, "I disconnected that phone machine and plugged in the computer modem, and hooked the modem to the laptop so I could look something up on *MEDLINE* without having to run over to the medical library."

"For the vascular surgery article," I remembered, and he nodded grimly.

"And," he said, "when I was finished I plugged the answering machine back in, and while I was at it I untangled the telephone cord, too."

Slowly I nodded; this much made perfect sense. We have only one telephone in our house as I feel a three-to-one ratio between human beings and intrusive electronic devices is really more than decent odds. But the phone is equipped with sixty feet of flexible cord so that anyone who desires to converse in privacy can simply pick up the blasted instrument and go somewhere else with it.

Somehow the cord gets more and more tangled, though—my own theory being that any household wire when left to itself makes a sort of furtive snake-like movement, tying itself eventually in a perfect clove hitch if not in a double Windsor—until after a while the only private place a person can go with that telephone is behind the lobster kettle at the rear of the pots and pans cabinet, or possibly into the refrigerator.

"Have a look," Solli invited. The answering machine's cord was now looped twice around the device's electrical cable, a situation I doubted any piece of household wiring no matter how unnaturally active could produce on its own.

"You didn't?" I began questioningly to Joey again.

"Nope. It sure looks like someone's been messing with it, all right. Boy, and I never even heard a thing," he enthused. "You think maybe it was the killer?"

He turned to me, eyes positively shining with the dramatic possibilities of this, and since as a matter of fact it was exactly what I thought I smiled and said of course not, we were all just getting ourselves way too overexcited and worried. A reasonable explanation was sure to turn up, I said, when we all calmed down and thought logically about it.

"Oh, logic," said Joey dismissively, "there's no fun in that." Then he put the telephone in his lap and wheeled off with it, to call up his friends and tell them a murderer had been in his house.

When he was gone I looked at Solli again. "Owen," I said, "has been with us since yesterday afternoon, and since he got to New Hampshire before us he must have started out before we did, too."

Solli nodded. Owen at the moment was crashed out on the sofa in the living room while David Fischer sprawled in a similar state of exhaustion on one of the overstuffed chairs. Just to mix things up a little I'd had the two of them drive back together while Phileta rode with us, and she was now sound asleep on our bed.

"And to get there when they did," I went on, "David and Phileta had to leave here in the middle of the night."

She'd simply wanted to talk to someone who wasn't being paid to listen, she said. When I wasn't at home, she'd gone to a diner where she learned about Symonds's death from the late television news, and that blew away what self-possession she still had; after all, she was still feeling rather fragile, and now someone else who'd hated Bell had gotten murdered.

That, at any rate, was how she'd told it. Why she hadn't thought Fischer himself might be dangerous— he'd had, after all, his own fairly well-known motives for killing Bell—was something neither he nor she had explained, and this bothered me considerably, since it seemed to me the only way she could know for sure that Fischer wasn't a murderer was for her to be one herself.

I did not, however, think that I would wake them to ask them this; silence, it seemed to me, was getting more golden by the minute and the longer it lasted, the less likely I was to have a bona fide nervous breakdown of my very own.

Besides, if one of them was guilty then one of them would lie to me, and I would still have no idea which one it was.

Sooner or later someone would have to go back for Owen's car, but as I doubted anyone would spy out his license plates in the valet parking lot of the Mount Washington Hotel that was probably the best place for it, for now at any rate.

"Someone," Solli pointed out, "could have called the lobby desk from inside the hotel, and left the message."

I pulled out the slip of paper and looked at it. HE CAN'T RUN was all it said, but that had been enough to bring me racing back here to check on Joey when I could not get him on the phone.

"But no one," he went on, "could have unplugged that phone machine and still be at the hotel with us, or have plugged it in again, and at the same time be driving back when we were."

"Unless," I mused, "someone got someone else to do it for them. To shift suspicion, knowing we'd realize that anyone who was with us couldn't possibly also be—"

Solli shook his head. "Hire a housebreaker to get in here, send us the note, disconnect the phone just long enough for us to call it and get worried, then get back in here again some time afterwards to hook it up again? I can't buy that, Charlotte. How could they be sure Joey wouldn't be sitting here eating breakfast or something? It would be too dicey, all the timing is too neat."

"The whole thing," I complained, "is too neat. It clears all three of them," I jerked my head toward the living room, "too well. Which to my mind means it doesn't clear any of them at all, because it's way too convenient for one of them."

"Even," Solli asked gently, "Owen?"

"Even Owen," I replied. "Because look, Solli, if I don't suspect him as hard as I do all the others, then I can't possibly remove suspicion from him convincingly, can I? I mean, if I'm just letting him off the hook all the time because it's with him that I sympathize the most."

I sat down sadly at the kitchen table. "Besides, he did hate Bell, and he did have the gun. And maybe all that about being so worried and helpless was only a ruse. I did call him first, you know. Mike Malley was right about that."

Thinking of Malley reminded me of another unpleasant thing. "By the way, you don't happen to know anything about Mike Malley's medical history, do you? He hasn't had his coronaries reamed out lately, or anything? Because I thought he was looking kind of cheesey yesterday. Even cheesier than usual, I mean.

"When," I added unhappily, "he was checking out the story of Owen standing over Reggie's croaked corpse with still another murder weapon. One, I might add, that has not yet been retrieved."

I hadn't even thought to ask Owen what he did with that gun, I realized embarrassedly. Probably he had it in his pocket right now.

"Um, no," Solli said. "No gossip around the hospital that I recall. Only, Charlotte, you're ignoring the main question here, I think. The question of why someone wanted you to come home."

"Oh, I'm not ignoring it at all. It's perfectly obvious to me, that part. Someone wanted me back in target range."

I looked at Solli. "After all, maintaining a large, fertile pool of suspects while diverting suspicion away from himself—or herself—seems to be the name of someone's game, wouldn't you say? If I died up there or had another horrid prank played on me, it would really pretty much have to be one of you four—although of course I do absolve you of suspicion in advance, my dear. If you wanted to kill me you could just do it the way you always do, with kindness."

Solli came over and began to massage the back of my neck in the manner he generally employs when he knows that I am flat up against it, but he doesn't want to get all sappy about it.

"Poor Charlotte," he said soothingly. "Should I take you away from all this? I still could, you know."

"Where?" I retorted. "Sorry, kiddo, you're just not built to be a crutch—as I've informed you many times in the past."

His fingers increased their gentle probing. "And what," he inquired leadingly, "am I built to be?"

Solli knew very well the answer to that, and in my exhausted and pliable state I was not about to resist allowing him to demonstrate that he knew it. Unfortunately, however, just as I was about to fall limp and utterly suggestible into his arms the typist came in, looking bright and infuriatingly perky as usual.

"Is everything all right with the phone?" she asked, putting down a pile of manuscript the approximate height of the Eiffel Tower.

I stared at the typist whom I had entirely forgotten was here, and then I stared at her manuscript. This, I gathered, was what she had written since yesterday, a production rate which immediately made me want to chain her to a typing chair and set her to cranking out romance novels. Since her trick apparently lay in pretending someone else had written her stuff and she was only retyping it, and since as far as I could tell romance novels already all read as if someone else had written them at least 500 times, I figured that at five grand a pop she could make us all millionaires in something under six weeks.

"What about the telephone?" I asked, still gazing at that enormous pile of paper and imagining what I could do if only I could pretend even half so well. Bye-bye home help books; hello, Hollywood. Then her words sank in and I sat up straight.

"Something wrong with the telephone? You mean, while you were here this morning?"

"Uh-huh," she said unconcernedly, reaching out to square up the stack of finished pages. "Well, not wrong, actually. Just that the telephone company repairman called and asked me to help him test the line. I'm sorry if I got it tangled up a little."

"How exactly did he test it?" Solli asked.

"Oh, it was simple," she assured him. "He just said would I please not answer it for half an hour or so because it would only be him making it ring. And when he was done he called back and said everything was fine, I could reconnect the answering machine if I had one, and thanks very much. Joey," she added, "was down in the basement doing laundry. I don't think he even knew I was here."

She looked from one to the other of us. "Wasn't that okay? Should I not have done that about the phone?"

"It's perfectly okay," I said, "you did absolutely right. Now, how about taking your work back into Solli's room—see if you can figure out how many layout sheets we still need to fill, now that we've got all this stuff of yours on hand."

"Okay," she said and went off to do just that. Watching her go I thought again that if only I could get her cloned, all my troubles would be over.

Or most of them would be over, anyway. "So that's how it worked," I said to Solli. "All done by telephone, easy as pie."

"Uh-huh," he said, frowning. "Listen, I think you ought to start being extremely careful. Somebody, if you ask me is—"

"Several sandwiches short of a picnic," I finished for him. "Don't worry, I'm going to stay here and work on the magazine and that damned table of contents. And since no one else seems to be going anywhere, there'll be plenty of witnesses around to tell you who to rip limb from limb in case anybody tries anything on me before you get back."

This of course did not quite satisfy Solli, who knows that I can get into deep and serious trouble just as well in my own home as anywhere else. Nevertheless he thought he ought to go over to the hospital to check on a couple of his patients, so he went off to change clothes with his face already settling into its serious doctor-type expression, which no matter what anyone else says is what I think they really pay them all that money for. Shortly thereafter, he went out.

Meanwhile Joey was in his room talking on the telephone, the typist was dummying up a set of layout sheets, and my impromptu house-guests were all asleep, all of which gave me the perfect opportunity to enjoy five minutes of silence, for heaven's sake, though I knew my actual chances of achieving this hovered somewhere between zilch and nada. And sure enough just as I sat down at the kitchen table with a fresh cup of coffee, some newly-sharpened pencils, and a sheet of notebook paper—I might, I thought, just as well try giving that table of contents a whack— someone started hammering on the downstairs back door.

"I've got it," the typist called pleasantly, and of course I did not tell her to go find Owen's gun and just shoot whoever it was. Moments later, though, I very much wished that I had as in stumbled Brady Willamette, looking apoplectic.

"Where," he demanded, spying the luggage still lined up in the back hall, "do you think you're going? And what's the idea of not answering your telephone?"

I looked at the typist. "It did ring a lot," she said.

Brady's face was red, his hair disheveled and his glasses askew. He stomped around the kitchen with his brow furrowed and his lip thrust out, favoring each appliance and item of furniture with a suspicious look before whirling belligerently on me.

"I don't like this. I don't like you sneaking off somewhere without telling me. You found something out, I'll bet, something important, too, and I want to know what it is right now."

"Brady," I said tiredly, "why don't you just sit down before I sit you down, and shut up before I shut you up."

"Don't you tell me what to do," he yelled, looking as if any minute he might fling himself on the kitchen floor kicking his heels and pounding his fists. "I want to know, I want to, do you hear me? And you've got to—"

Calmly I ran a glass of water at the kitchen sink and began pouring it in a steady stream over Brady Willamette's head. He stiffened, spluttered, and abruptly stopped making stupid noises.

"You," I told him, "are a nincompoop. You have no brains, no judgment, no manners, and no business barging in here to—"

But Brady was not listening to me. He was staring at the doorway that led into the living room, a doorway entirely filled by the large blinking sleep-befuddled form of Owen Strathmore.

"Oh," said Brady. "Oh, I get it—you're hiding him. I saw his picture in the paper, the guy they think killed Wes."

Drawing himself up importantly to his full height of nearly five-feet-five, he strutted to where Owen stood. Reaching up, he poked his index finger into Owen's chest.

"Did you," he demanded, "kill my friend Wes Bell?"

Owen frowned and passed a hand over his eyes as if hoping he might still be asleep, and when he woke up this obnoxious little wombat would have vanished back to wherever bad dreams go.

"No," he muttered, "I didn't."

"Are you *sure*?" Brady asked insistently, still poking at Owen's shirt front. "Because he was going to help me, you know. He said I was a talented, a *gifted* young writer of extremely important—"

"Brady," I said urgently, watching Owen's face. "I don't think you'd better..."

Frowning in puzzlement at the finger that just kept poking while Brady Willamette kept quacking, Owen at last reached down and seized the offending digit firmly in his big hand, and began turning it this way and that as if trying to decide what to do with it.

"Hey!" Brady squealed as Owen's other hand reached around, finding its way to the back of Brady's collar. "Hey, you big ox, you let go of me! My father is an important guy in this town, darn it, you can't just—hey!"

Then Brady made his unwisest move of all, rearing back for a too-short roundhouse swing at Owen Strathmore who in spite of his emotional helplessness was still physically quite a large and powerful man.

Lifting Brady by his shirt-back, without strain or apparent effort Owen raised the squirming little pest until his shoes at last parted company with my kitchen linoleum.

"Wah!" blurted Brady Willamette, back-pedaling in thin air.

"Charlotte," Owen inquired, "was there anywhere special you wanted me to put this?"

"Put him down, Owen," I said.

Brady's feet herky-jerked high off the floor, his arms pumping wildly and his breath coming in thin little sobs through which a few words could still be distinguished.

"Help. . . glurp. . . *wah!*" Brady Willamette said.

"You're sure?" Owen asked me solicitously again. "I can put him," he added, "anywhere I want to put him. So you just let me know if there's someplace in particular. . ."

"Down, please," I said. "Right there in front of you."

"Glurk," Brady agreed, beginning to turn blue.

"Okay." Owen opened his hand and Brady dropped. "Don't poke me again," Owen advised him mildly. "I'm not in the mood for it."

Then he turned and wandered back to the living room, the sofa's springs protesting as he fell back down upon it.

"Doomed," his foghorn voice came disconsolately. "Utterly, completely, thoroughly, unsalvageably—doomed."

Meanwhile Brady's face as he clambered from the floor was dark and threatening as a thundercloud. Watching him I thought that unless I could distract him somehow—and fast—he was going to rain on a lot more parades besides Owen Strathmore's. Prison garb certainly would put a crimp in my fashion sense, for instance—last I heard, the harboring of a fugitive was felony material—and somewhere right now a shirt whose sleeves tied firmly in the back was being tailored for Phileta Poole. In fact, I doubted whether any of our problems could be solved by the sudden arrival of a police SWAT team, and that was just what was going to happen as soon as Brady Willamette got hold of the nearest telephone.

" . . . savage," he gasped, climbing onto a kitchen chair.

"Brady," I said, refilling that water glass and handing it to him. "Calm down, now, Brady, you know Owen is under a lot of strain lately, and I really don't think it was very wise of you to . . ."

" . . . witnesses," Brady choked out, yanking his collar and swallowing some of the water. "I'll show him who he's dealing with, he thinks he can make some kind of monkey out of me..."

Personally I thought Brady Willamette's monkey-hood was well established, and could probably not be altered by anything short of genetic code revision. Still, he was an extremely pathetic character and besides I had to stop him somehow.

"...*gifted*," he spluttered, which of course was the magic word if only I knew how to pronounce it.

"Brady," I tried once more, thinking that if this did not work I might as well just go lie down on the sofa beside Owen and wait for the sound of jackboots thumping up the front steps.

"Brady, how would you like to become the assistant editor of a major nationally distributed magazine?"

Bingo.

TWENTY MINUTES LATER I had them all up and assembled around the kitchen table.

"I'm fed up," I told them. "I'm tired of the lot of you absorbing all my time and energy. If it weren't for you—" I waved my hand at the papers and envelopes, the written and half-written articles, and the layout sheets like big stiff sections of graph paper laid out before me "—if it weren't for you I could get all this work done myself. So instead, you all are going to help me."

With varying degrees of enthusiasm they agreed this was fair and accepted the tasks I had set out for them.

"You," I told Phileta, "are going to write an eight-page essay explaining what an important literary critic like yourself looks for in a piece of fiction. What makes it good or bad. In words," I added, "of two syllables or less."

"You," I told Owen, "are going to teach *Pen and Pencil*'s readers how to create an action hero, so they can all grow up to be cheap-shot write-for-hire purveyors of mindlessly violent pulp-novel series adventures just like you. If, of course, they turn out to have the talent for it."

"Doesn't take talent," Owen muttered. "Takes boneheaded stubbornness and a good thesaurus, that's all." But he sat down at the table and pulled a loose-leaf pad toward him nevertheless.

"And you," I told David Fischer, "are going to let the typist here show you how to calculate column-inches, so you can help figure out where to put the spillovers and how big to blow up the cartoons and the author's photographs—" I handed Brady Willamette a file folder "—while the assistant editor here picks the cover art out of a bunch of illos I've got all assembled for him."

Brady frowned at the file folder. "That's not a job for an editor. I thought I was supposed to be in charge of—"

"Delegate," I whispered to him, "always delegate. You can't keep an eye on the whole process if you're sweating the details."

"Right," he whispered back, "right, I'll make sure they don't start slacking off. But—what are *you* going to do?"

"Well, Brady," I said aloud, "now that the entire magazine is safely in your capable hands—" from behind him in the doorway Joey rolled his eyes toward heaven, no doubt begging forgiveness on my behalf for all the big fat lies I was telling "—I think I deserve an hour or so of rest and relaxation. So I'm going out to visit an old girlfriend of mine."

This last was the biggest lie of all since Corinna Bell was certainly no friend of mine, a visit to her would be neither restful nor relaxing, and if she ever heard me describing her as old she would have my heart out on a platter.

Still I definitely did intend to see her, for two reasons.

Joey's excellent manners extended not only to persons calling, but also to persons with whom any callers wished to speak—in this case, me. On the counter by the telephone right now lay a list of the people who had called—and gotten through—while I was at the Mount Washington Hotel. All the callers except Corinna Bell were sitting right this minute in my very own kitchen, however, which meant that:

(a) Corinna would have known where to send that threatening message about Joey, simply because Joey had told her, and

(b) I wasn't keeping completely solid tabs on her, a situation I thought might just as well be rectified at once.

This was the first reason I wanted to see her. The other came from a remark of David Fischer's. " . . . because you'd had an affair with her," he'd told

Owen, "or because you didn't have, I'm not sure which."

Seeing Corinna's name now reminded me and made me wonder again—how had the cops gotten hold of Owen's letter to her so fast, anyway?

Certainly it was convenient for the police, having it in hand so quickly—and maybe even more convenient for somebody else. But according to Owen, Corinna said that the letter had disappeared and she was afraid her husband had it. Assuming that was so, Bell might have given it over to the authorities before he got murdered, on account of the threat it contained. But then Owen would surely have been contacted by the police, and warned to stop making the threats—this being the only sensible reason for Bell to have lodged such a complaint in the first place. Also according to Owen, however, he had not heard from the police until after Wes Bell's murder.

Another possibility was that someone else had had the letter—not Wes Bell and not Corinna, either. Someone, perhaps, who had stolen it meaning to use it for blackmail, then given it to the police instead. But this idea also did not quite make sense, as Bell's death would most certainly have made such a letter more valuable, not less, and even if it didn't up the ante any blackmailer worth his or her salt would certainly have kept it anyway, not obligingly surrendered it to assist in a murder investigation.

All of which to my mind left Corinna, who was already one of the most inveterate and creative liars I had ever met in my life. So: what if the letter had never really disappeared? What if it was Corinna who gave it to the police?

Thinking this, I left my houseguests scribbling and pasting, snipping and measuring under the tactfully laid-back direction of the typist; none of them, I thought, would be likely to try doing anything weird while being watched by all the rest.

"These are awful," Brady complained as I passed through the kitchen for the final time, "don't you have any other art we can use?"

He really was the most offensive little twit. "I'll stop at the office on my way back," I promised him, "and see if we've got anything else that might come up to your high standards."

Unfazed, Brady nodded frowningly at me. Meanwhile Joey was getting ready to head over to Myron Rosewater's, as except for apologetic visits to my house Myron was still grounded for three more weeks. To cheer him up Joey was bringing him some pizza and a new issue of *Penny Stock Digest*. We parted at the end of the front walk. I told him to be careful, he told me the same, and I walked very quickly the fifteen blocks to the station, just making the train to Manhattan. As far as I could figure, there were just two reasons why Corinna Bell should have handed Owen's letter over to the police and gotten him in so much trouble. The first was that Corinna believed Owen really had murdered her husband, and the second was that she'd murdered him herself.

Either way I was going to get to the bottom of it. I had no money and no privacy, no new issue of *Pen and Pencil* and little hope of drumming up one. I

didn't even have a decent staff since the poet and Wes
Bell were dead, and I hardly thought the typist would
be sticking around very much longer, now that she'd
found out she could make up new stuff faster than
most people could copy old stuff.

On top of it all I felt absolutely no certainty whatsoever that the next time I reached into my mailbox I
would not find a venomous snake or a black-widow
spider, or perhaps some cunning arrangement of rusty
nails painted with nice fresh botulism just waiting in
the darkness to be grasped by me.

Corinna was lying about the letter, I was certain of
it. My only question was why, and when I saw her she
was going to answer it. Otherwise, I was going to grab
her by those delicate-looking collarbones of hers and
shake her until the truth fell out of her mouth like a set
of cheap false teeth.

"WHY, CHARLOTTE, what a nice surprise," Corinna
gushed.

"I thought you might enjoy a little company," I said
as she stepped back reluctantly from the door to let me
in. "And I was in the neighborhood."

The apartment was one of those vast old pre-war
jobs with high ceilings, hand-carved moldings and
cornices, and room enough to house a family of fourteen. Alone in it Corinna must have felt like a marble
rattling around in a box.

"Keeping busy, I see." I looked around. The enormous parlor window flanked by maroon draperies
looked straight out over Central Park. Through a
shifting spring-green canopy of leaves the early-

afternoon light fell on cardboard cartons, manila file folders, shoeboxes full of envelopes, scraps, and receipts.

"Yes," Corinna laughed a little uncertainly. "I decided to try organizing things a bit. No point in keeping all of it, might as well sort the trash from the treasures."

The sight gave me a chill: manuscripts heaped on the floor and strewn across the furniture, novels in manuscript boxes and short stories paper-clipped, all scattered fragments of a snuffed-out creative life.

Sorting them, my great-aunt-Fanny. Here the guy was barely cold and Corinna was preparing to turn a quick buck on the contents of his file cabinets, assembling a hasty smorgasbord for literary vultures while he was still posthumously profitable.

"You know," I said, "you're going about this all wrong."

Her pretty face crinkled in pretended hurt. She was wearing a grey velour jumpsuit with pink cuffs and collar, bright pink buttons down the front and pink Reeboks. "Why, I can't imagine what you—"

"Selling off his stuff," I told her, "like it was odd lots of junk at a garage sale."

I picked up a handful of pages and let them fall. "I just hope you haven't let anyone else in here. You'll get pennies on the dollar if people find out how much of this there is—you've got to make the marketplace think Wes Bell material is scarce."

She nodded in cautious calculation. "You mean offer one or maybe two a time," she said slowly. "Let it trickle out?"

"In dribs and drabs," I agreed. "Wes's agent will know how to handle it, but don't dump the whole shebang's worth even on him. Just pretend it's your virginity, Corinna. You used to dangle that like a perfumed hanky, you ought to remember how."

She flushed, but I could see she got the point.

"I should have known you'd be expert in the grit and grime of commerce, Charlotte. The lower aspects of culture always were your *metier*. Any other suggestions? Because if not, I'm afraid I'm just a hair's breadth too busy for—"

"Tell me about your affair with Owen Strathmore, Corinna. Were you or weren't you with Owen when Wes died?"

At that her cheeks went a brighter pink than the buttons on her shirt. She opened her mouth but I forged on ahead of her.

"Come on, Corinna, let your hair down for once in your life. Wouldn't it be a relief just to cut the crap for five minutes?"

She stalked to the door, opened it. "As I said, you always were a crude person. I really think you'd better—"

"Not as crude," I said, "as what the gossip columnists are going to write about you when the story comes out—which it will at the trial. Your name's going to be pond-scum when they get through with you. No one's going to believe you weren't involved with Owen. I'm sure the police don't believe it now, they're just playing you along."

I walked to the window. Down in the park a woman was being drawn along by a brace of small poodles on red leather leashes, yapping and pulling every which way.

"What they'll believe," I said, "is that you sacrificed your lover to save yourself—that the two of you killed Wes together and now you're trying to make it look as if Owen did it alone."

"That's ridiculous." She frowned pettishly; any minute she would stomp her widdle footsie. "I haven't done anything wrong."

"Oh, of course not, that's why you turned a threatening letter of Owen's over to the cops the minute Wes got blown away. Juicy, Corinna—very juicy. The tabloids are going to love it, too. You'll make Leona Helmsley look like Mother Theresa."

"Unless," I added, "you want my advice on how to manage your publicity. You know you're going to get the publicity, don't you? The only question now is how you get it. Nice or not-nice, but for sure."

She'd turned away as I said this last bit, but now she turned back to me again with her pretty face all creased and reddened like a flower someone had crumpled in a fist.

"He was a bastard," she whispered. "My husband, the writer. What a perfect sonofabitch he was. I wish I'd shot him myself."

Interesting, although not totally believable; the part about not having shot him, that is. Her voice was plenty murderous.

"I've heard he could be difficult," I prodded tactfully.

"Difficult?" Her laugh was a sound like wet silk ripping. "Wes Bell raised mental cruelty to an art form—and not only to his wife."

His wife. Suddenly Corinna didn't look any more like the spoiled rich bitch I'd always loved to hate. Instead she looked like a frail pretty woman who'd traded hard all her life on the only coin she had—her looks, her money, and an unfoolable eye for the main chance—and had come out on the short end without understanding why. Around us the apartment was silent as an upholstered tomb, and she seemed to hear it, too.

"He said it was only because people wanted to take advantage of him and he had to defend himself, but he loved it. He loved having his old friends ask favors, like little dogs begging for scraps from the master's table. He loved making them squirm and crawl, not that they were any better—"

She cocked a hip and put on a pleading expression. "Oh, Wes, introduce me to your editor. Oh, Wes, refer me to an agent," she simpered. "God. The dance of the happy sycophants."

Her look hardened. "And he adored saying no to them. How could he be sure he was up if they weren't down? God, he was a miserable bastard.

"And you love it, too, I'll bet," she said as she turned abruptly on me. "Lo, how the mighty hath fallen, I'm sure it all just amuses you tremendously. It's exactly the kind of thing a person like you enjoys—plenty of flash and trash."

It occurred to me with this remark that Corinna really was much more astute than I had given her credit for—which was why I continued suspecting her even while I felt sorry for her.

She sank into one of her beautifully-proportioned polished chintz armchairs, looking like a rag doll that somebody had just yanked all the stuffing out of.

"Well you can take your amusement," her voice began falling apart, "and you can *take* your reader interest, your book-club deals and your goddamned foreign-language sub*sid*iary rights—"

"Corinna," I put in as gently as I could; I'd always thought she was hard as nails but now here she was coming apart right in front of me.

"Corinna, are you trying to tell me that you loved him?"

She looked up, and in her swimmingly lovely violet eyes I saw what was for her the terrible unerasable bottom line.

"Why couldn't he love me back?" she asked in the voice of a mystified and bereaved little girl. "He was the only one I ever really wanted. Why couldn't he just want me, too?"

"And that," I said, "was how you got involved with Owen. He wanted you very much, didn't he? Admired you, adored you, even." And still did, I thought, remembering his voice when he talked about her. In spite of everything he still did.

"Yes." Her headful of glossy curls shone in the light from the big window behind her. "Owen's such an ox. But he pursued me, he harassed me like some lovesick teenager. That letter—you can't imagine how ridiculous it was. But I was lonely, he caught me at a low moment . . ."

She paused, and when she went on her voice had recovered its standard uncaring brittleness. "I had to break it off with him. He was amusing for awhile but if anyone ever found out I'd be an utter laughing-stock. So I told him the letter was missing and I thought Wes had found it, that I was afraid and I couldn't see him any more for a while. That was on the morning Wes was killed."

"But the letter wasn't missing. In fact you must have had it with you in New Haven, and when you found out Wes was dead you took it to the police. Why, Corinna?"

"I kept all Owen's letters with me all the time. Too horrid, if anyone else should find them. I simply couldn't risk that."

She shrugged. "And I gave it to the police because Owen wouldn't take no for an answer. I could see I was going to have trouble with him, and with Wes out of the picture I knew he would be even more insistent. So I had to do something, didn't I?"

She asked this as if it were the most reasonable thing in the world.

"You made Owen into a murder suspect," I said slowly, "just to get him out of your way?"

"Well," she said, as if I were being rather stupid, "and to make the police see I wasn't a suspect—so they'd see I was on their side."

All I could do was stare at her. "Corinna, what time was it when you left Owen?"

She told me. If she could be believed—and just this once I thought that she could—then Corinna Bell wasn't merely the woman who had made Owen

Strathmore a murder suspect. She was also his only alibi, and he was hers. "Corinna, you're going to have to tell them the truth, and I think you'd better do it now."

Her chin went up stubbornly. "No. Why should I? It's his word against mine. No one ever saw us together, I made sure of that. I don't have to tell anybody anything.

"And if you do," she added in dangerous tones, "I'll be sure to make you extremely sorry. You know I can do it, too, don't you? I have a lot of friends. Philip Poole, for example, is a dear acquaintance of mine. You'll end up writing classified ads."

There, that was the Corinna we knew and loved: bitchy, bossy, and endowed with all the high moral principles of an alley-cat.

She laughed, a sharp brittle sound like a piece of expensive crystal being shattered. "I can tell you all my little secrets, can't I, Charlotte? So relaxing, to confide in someone one knows won't say a word—because you are nothing but a money-grubbing little hackwriter, dear, and you can't afford to lose the work I can keep you from getting. I can do it with a few phone calls."

She could, too, because Corinna made it her business to have things on people. They did her favors so she wouldn't rat on them, make their private pains into amusing little anecdotes she could tell at cocktail parties.

Or so she wouldn't ruin them with a few phone calls.

Down in the park the woman with the poodles was on her knees trying to straighten out the red leather leashes. But the more she tried to unbraid them the more tangled they grew. The little dogs' pink mouths showed as they yapped and danced excitedly. Watching, I thought about just letting Corinna go down the tubes. It was what she deserved, and it was what she was going to get: somewhere, someone had to have seen her with Owen. Three-hundred-pound bald men in lumber shirts and overalls, after all, do tend to stick in the memories of even bored, burnt-out hotel desk clerks and cocktail waitresses. When Owen's lawyer found one of them Corinna was dead in the believability department. If she weren't so utterly stupidly self-absorbed, she'd have realized that. So why not keep quiet? Probably Owen's lawyer had his own investigators checking out Owen's story. Soon Corinna would be too busy scrambling for her own foothold to worry about making the earth crumble beneath my feet. The trouble was that if she didn't get me now she'd get me later; she had a long memory, especially for grudges.

"If you tell the truth right now," I said quietly, "all the sensation will be over in a couple of days. If you wait, or even make them put you on the witness stand, it'll last for weeks."

"I won't be here. I'm going to Switzerland for a rest."

Typical Corinna: hit and run. Slowly I walked to her chair, picked up some pages from the table by it and glanced unseeingly at them. What the hell, maybe it was for the best. If I couldn't get hired freelance I'd have plenty of time to write that novel I was always whining about, wouldn't I?

"Corinna, either you tell or I'm going to. Now, today."

Her glossy head swung up in astonishment. "You betraying little gutter rat, I told you those things in confidence. You keep your filthy mouth shut, or I'll—"

"Right," I said. "I know. You'll ruin me."

Her face was blotched and ugly with fury, too terrible to look into for very long. I glanced away from it to the papers in my hand, and that was when I saw what was written on them.

"Corinna," I said hastily, "I take it all back. Just don't do anything, don't go anywhere, and don't talk to anyone until I call you, all right?"

I headed for the door at a sprint. "Maybe you don't have to be gossip-meat after all," I called over my shoulder at her.

"Are you insane? What—"

"These letters," I waved them, "they're Wes's, but they're copies. Do you know where the originals are?"

Corinna squinted. "I think Wes took them to New Haven with him, but I'm not sure. The police haven't given me back all his things, yet. They're from that gauche little pest, that—"

"I know. Brady Willamette." I yanked open the apartment door. "Remember, Corinna, sit tight and shut up, and I'll call you as soon as I can."

Slamming the door on her questions I ran for the elevator, scanning the sheaf of letters again as I ham-

mered the "down" button and heard the old mecha-
nism clankingly engage.

The car descended with the slowness of a bad
dream, the kind where someone is chasing you and
you run, but somehow you aren't getting anywhere.
Out in the street I dashed for a phone booth, found it
out of order and raced down the avenue two blocks to
the next one.

Lieutenant Mike Malley wasn't in; the desk ser-
geant didn't know where he was, or when he would be
back. Yes, he would tell him I'd called but didn't know
when he would get the message.

Solli had gone to the OR with an emergency gas-
trectomy and wouldn't be out again for four hours or
more.

And the line was busy at home.

I slammed down the receiver, darted out in front of
a cab, and hammered on the hood to make it stop.

"Jeeze, lady," the driver said, "where'sa goddamn
fire?"

"New Haven," I gasped, falling into the back seat.
"Listen, whatever the dispatcher says is the fare, I'll
give you double—and *please* hurry, I think there's a
murderer in my house."

NINE

THERE WAS nothing to do in the back of the cab but
think, so I did. In my hands were dozens of letters
from Brady Willamette to Wes Bell, their dates span-
ning only about four weeks starting five weeks or so
before Wes died. As I looked through them again I
could see why Bell had kept copies of them. A few of
the earliest ones were pleasant enough: admire your
work, hope to meet you again sometime, blah-di-blah.
Quickly, though, the writer's friendliness deterio-
rated: subtle digs, obvious resentment progressing
rapidly to threats.

I guess we can't all be lucky enough to hit it big like
you, Brady wrote fairly early on, who did you have to
pay off, ha-ha? Later: I saw you out drinking with all
your important editor freinds (that was how Brady
spelled it). I guess it didn't occur to you to invite me,
I'm not a big deal writer like you with lots of contacts
and publisity (sic), am I? And: I don't see why you
can't help me. Why won't you help me? You don't
deserve your sucsess (Brady's spelling again).

Then there was a short break, followed by a note so
chummy and sticky-sweet it felt as if it were written on
fly-paper: thanks for the lunch and good advice.

Apparently Wes had tried getting rid of Brady by
humoring him. Which of course was a mistake; in two
days Brady was back, nastier and more explicit than

before, complaining that his phone calls were not being returned and what about the manuscripts he sent, had Wes read them yet or showed them to any editors?

And finally, real trouble: As you can see from enclosed photos I know everywhere you go & do, & also your ugley (Brady) wife. I don't deserve the way your (sic) treating me, I know things you would not like told. Next time I call you should answer, it wouldn't kill you to do me one simple favor. And more in the same vein (or vien, as Brady spelled it in threatening to slit his own if Wes continued ignoring him) until five days before I found Bell dead.

"Driver," I said, "could you please pull over at the next service plaza? I need to make a call."

He groused a little, but he did it. I left him listening to Art Rust Junior on Sports Talk radio, humoring some guy who could manage the Yankees better himself, fah Chrissake.

"Joey," I said when he answered, "put Brady on, will you?"

"He's gone home," he said. "He got mad when the typist told him to keep his cotton-pickin' blue pencil off her typescript. He said she was fired, and she said she was fired when *you* said so, not him. Then she called him a bossy pipsqueak. So he left."

I sighed. Still, it might have been a lot worse: Joey could have been there alone with Brady. "Okay, look up his number and read it to me. Are the rest still there?"

"Uh-huh." He read me the number. "They're getting ready to go eat, though. David's trying to talk Phileta into eating, too."

"You tell Phileta I said do it, and you go along, all right? Are they going somewhere your chair can get in?"

Then another thought hit me, the obvious one. "Wait a minute, you mean Owen's going out?"

"Uh-huh." Joey's voice went sober. "I asked him wasn't he scared to go where people would see him but he says he's a man, not a mouse, and if there's no ramp he'll toss me on his shoulder like a sack of oats. I don't know, though, Charlotte, I'm not sure it's such a good idea with the cops looking for him and all."

Good old Owen, he must be getting his wind back. Good old Joey, too, for being such a sport—although if Owen meant to stroll around with his bare face hanging out I'd better work fast before some good citizen noticed him and summoned the gendarmes. Not that I had a lot of choice. Every minute Brady was running loose was a minute to the bad, as far as I was concerned.

"Fine," I told Joey. "If Owen runs into any trouble, tell him I said not to worry, I'll get it all straightened out, okay? And then you just hang back."

He snorted. "Yeah, what else would I do, run away?"

I paused over this, decided his sarcasm was healthy and let it pass without comment.

"And when Solli gets home you just stick with him until I get there," I finished.

"Why?" His voice quickened with interest. "Is something going on?"

"Just go along with your tired old stepmother on this one. I'll fill you in on all the details when I get home."

With grudging good humor Joey agreed to indulge me in my age and rapidly advancing decrepitude, whereupon I punched in Brady's number and Mrs. Willamette answered.

"Yes," she said doubtfully, "I think he's here. Who shall I say is calling?"

"Tell him it's his editor," I said; that ought to bring him on the run. But she returned sounding more doubtful than before.

"I don't understand," she said in the puzzled, faintly hurt tones of a mother whose son might as well be an alien from outer space for all she really knew about him any more.

"His computer and the television are on," she said, "and his printer is printing, but—"

In other words it sounded as if he were home when he wasn't, which no doubt suited Brady's purposes admirably; fewer questions from dear old Mom.

"That's all right," I told her. "If he comes in, would you tell him Charlotte would like to see him down at the office—" I glanced at my watch— "around eight-thirty?"

That ought to give me time to pick up a blank tape and load it into my cassette-recorder. It was the one Joey gave me when it proved unequal to the brain-curdling decibel levels he favored, but I thought it would pick up Brady Willamette's confession well enough—assuming I proved equal to the task of extracting it, which was my next project.

"Well, I'm not sure," Mrs. Willamette said worriedly. "That will be after dark, won't it? Brady probably won't even have finished eating his—"

"Mrs. Willamette?" I broke in gently. *Mrs. Willamette, I'm going to trap your boy and send him where the walls are high and the crayons are blunt, and people in white jackets will study him for the rest of his life as if he were a strange bug*—"Just tell him, will you please?" I said.

She must have heard something in my voice, because there was a silence in which I was certain she knew what I was thinking.

"Yes, dear," she replied quietly at last. "I'll tell him."

"Okay," I said to the cab driver, "thanks."

He shrugged. "Your money. Still New Haven? Ain't decided Albany? Maybe Montreal? Hey, you got the dime, I got the time."

I shook my head. "Still New Haven." I gave him the address of the *Pen and Pencil* office. It was nearly five now and the traffic on the turnpike was heavy with the evening commute.

"Getcha there six-fifteen," he said as the cab shot up the ramp, cut off a highballing eighteen-wheeler and lurched across three lanes to the left one. Yanking the wheel he swerved into it, leaving a good ten inches to spare between us and an oncoming Greyhound whose air-horn trumpeted in outrage.

"Gah," I said as my life finished passing before my eyes. The driver glanced into the rear-view, amused.

"Don't worry, lady, I ain't gonna let you get killed. You ain't paid me yet."

Rats. That was what I had forgotten. All the money I could get hold of was in Solli's bureau drawer beneath his dress socks. Sighing, I told the driver I'd changed my mind again and gave him the Court Street address. He nodded as if this were little more than he had been expecting; it seemed that among members of his profession people who took impromptu cross-country taxicab trips were well-known not to have their acts together.

An hour and a half later we pulled up in front of the house and I ran inside. Solli's sock drawer was indeed well-furnished with green stuff; this I replaced with a hastily-scrawled IOU and raced back out to the cab again, snapping the porch lights on as I went since neither Solli nor anyone else was home yet.

It was just seven o'clock when I paid the driver and he let me out in front of the office brownstone, telling me I ought to watch out fah myself and gunning the cab away into the darkness.

The street was very quiet and I agreed emphatically with him as I watched his taillights go. Somehow until this moment it hadn't occurred to me that I was going to be sitting in an empty building with a certifiable fruitcake, and a murderous fruitcake at that, trying to drop a net around him. If the fruitcake made an appearance, of course.

Hurriedly I unlocked the downstairs door and switched on the fluorescents over the stairway landings, hearing my own footsteps loud in my ears as I went up. The faint buzz from the fluorescent fixtures was ominous and expectant-sounding, although I was sure this was only a product of my imagination.

Pretty sure, anyway. In my bag was the cassette recorder, loaded with a tape. The batteries were fresh and the machine would fit in my desk drawer; probably with the volume cranked the sound-quality would suck, but the words would be distinguishable. Good enough for the kind of performance I wanted to capture, at any rate: Brady Willamette's swan-song.

What the heck, all he wanted was to be a famous writer. And with the story he had to tell—a true-life murder account from the point of view of the murderer himself—he could do it in spades. At least, he could do the telling part. For the writing he would need a collaborator, someone who could actually put six words in a row without misspelling two of them. Someone who had an agent, experience, a couple of publishing contacts under the belt. Someone sympathetic and a little bit greedy, who wanted to help him for his own sake and for a percentage.

Me, for instance. So first I would get the tape-recorder all set up and then I would call Mike Malley and ask him to come on over here, back me up in case things didn't go exactly as I planned and arrest Brady for murder afterwards.

I supposed I could have just taken Brady's letters to Malley instead. Trouble was, they didn't prove anything by themselves. In the long run I felt certain they could get Owen off the hook, but the wheels of justice turneth exceedingly slow. Besides, the little son-ofabitch had killed the poet, not to mention Reggie Symonds, whose worst sin had been that he was boring, and Wes Bell who for all his flaws did not deserve a big hole blown in the middle of his forehead.

And he'd threatened Joey. Never mind that he hadn't done anything to him. That he'd mentioned it, that he'd even thought of it—that was plenty.

In short, Brady Willamette was mine. Or so I thought, anyway, until I unlocked my office door, flipped the overheads on, and found Brady already there sitting behind my desk.

"Charlotte," he said in toneless greeting. The pistol wasn't in his pocket, and he wasn't glad to see me. Not at all.

AMAZING WHAT A difference perspective can make. A weapon which when viewed from the side resembles little more than a toy gun can look like enough firepower to defend an aircraft carrier when you are staring down the barrel of it.

Brady got up from behind the desk and came over to me. "My mother said you left a message. I was glad to hear from you, I'd been calling around looking for you all afternoon."

Uh-oh. "Really?" I tried to keep my voice light. "You could have asked me where I was going to be, Brady, I'd have—"

He laughed mirthlessly. "I don't think so. How come you're such pals with Mrs. Bell? You didn't look too friendly with her the other night at the writers' workshop."

He gave the last two words an unpleasant twist. "You didn't know I'd been following you, did you?

All the time you've been laughing at me behind my back, but now I've got the last laugh."

He poked me with the gun. It didn't feel good. I'd have grabbed for it but Brady looked twitchy as a cat's whisker and I thought he would shoot me if I even breathed funny. Misery and confusion were coming off him in sour-smelling waves but he knew right where the trigger was, no confusion about that.

You can kill a person with a .22. Head, neck, heart, lung, liver: pick one. Murder isn't a rocket science—lucky for Brady but not so lucky for me—and you don't need an assault rifle.

"When I couldn't find you anywhere else I got a hunch," he said, "and what do you know? Mrs. Bell recognized my voice, too. She told me you'd just left and you were going to step on me like the disgusting worm I was, with copies of the letters I'd sent."

Dogs or people, it makes no difference: too much breeding makes for weakened brains as Corinna had proven once again, her and her damned big mouth.

"How'd you get the gun into Owen's gun room?"

I thought about trying to get my hand inside my bag, decided against this as the pressure of Brady's gun against my neck went up a notch. He was so wired to the eyes with his own adrenaline that he could probably feel what I was thinking right through his skin.

"Broke a cellar window," he said. "That dump, who'd notice? A couple of others were already broken, it turned out. He had a big bunch of keys hung by the cellar steps, so I tried them. I didn't know what was in that room, but I was sure glad when I found out.''

Why he'd picked Owen to take the blame was obvious; he hadn't only been following Wes Bell. He'd also been following Corinna in case her doings might give him something extra to hold over Bell's head. So with his special brand of lowlife weasel cunning he'd known just whom to nail for Wes's murder: Corinna's boyfriend. Owen's letter had just put the frosting on the cake, suspicion-wise; probably Brady hadn't even known about it.

In fact with everything falling together so neatly he'd had a remarkable streak of luck going for him lately, one I sincerely hoped was not going to continue. It looked like it just might, though, as Brady's hand went past me and snapped the office lights out.

''Come on,'' he said, nudging me into the hallway and closing the door behind us. ''We have places to go and people to see.''

''Which people are those?'' I kept trying to sound casual, as if he weren't a killer with a gun pressed hard against me, and it kept not working. Something about the situation made my mouth feel like a strip of beef jerky, all dry and puckery.

''The ones,'' he. replied, ''I'm going to get rid of while I'm getting rid of you.''

Left, right, left: Brady knew the fastest routes along the dark side streets. Twenty minutes later we were walking up Owen Strathmore's front walk.

The house was dark. I wondered if Anna was inside. ''What are we doing here?''

Brady laughed. "For starters, I'm going to go through the cellar window, come up, and open the door," he said.

"What keeps me from yelling my head off while you do?"

"Nothing. The crippled kid wouldn't like it, though. He's upstairs, and he wants to see you. Before he dies," Brady added, releasing me from his grip.

My shirt where he'd been holding me was sodden with sweat, but the chill I felt had nothing to do with the sudden rush of cool evening air on my skin.

Lying, I thought, he's lying to get me inside. "Brady," I began, "don't you see you're never going to get away with—"

"Shut up. This isn't about getting away with anything, it's about getting even. And," he added, "getting famous at the same time."

He moved back into the tangle of weeds and shrubbery growing close against Owen's house. "Because there's more than one way," he said, "to skin a cat."

His shape slid into the shadows; I heard him chuckle back there. An instant later something sailed from the darkness at me.

It was Joey's cap, the World Series souvenir cap he had bought last year with Solli in California. I picked it up and heard the front door unlocking. Then it swung wide and the long dark hall inside yawned at me like an open grave.

Dim light shone from a lamp at the top of the staircase. It made the figures in the wallpaper seem to creep. The treads creaked as Brady followed me up.

He'd chosen Owen's workroom for his base of operations, but the chamber was now almost unrecognizable: dozens of Owen's books flung to the floor, his notes torn and scattered everywhere, his typewriter smashed where Brady had flung it in a rage of envy.

In one corner against a pile of the torn-down heavy tapestry drapes lay Joey. He looked unhurt, but his eyes were dark with apology and his wrists were bound with the strapping-tape Owen used to seal up manuscript mailing boxes. His legs stuck awkwardly out at an angle that made me wince.

Piled beside him were the pieces of his wheelchair: wheels, seat, leg rests all stacked as if ready for packing in a crate.

"He came to the restaurant," Joey said. "The ramp was at a different entrance so he caught me alone there. He said you were over here, and you wanted me to come without telling the others."

His eyes turned to Brady, who was busily sweeping the last of Owen's papers off the big oaken table. "Only when we got in here he tipped me out of the chair and then I saw he had the gun."

I looked at him. "How did you get upstairs, on your hands?"

He nodded; I imagined him hauling himself step by step. "He said he had you up here already, he'd kill you if I didn't. Then he knocked me out and wrapped my wrists like this. I'm sorry, Charlotte, I shouldn't have believed him."

"Shut up," said Brady, his lip curling with distaste. "You, you're nothing but a defective punk anyway, why didn't you just wheel yourself in front of a train or something? Nothing but a cripple, you are, only not for much longer.''

Joey's eyes widened, but not at the threat. He knew it was only an act, just an attitude Brady had copped from some gangster movie he'd seen at four in the morning in his mother's basement. He didn't like what Brady called him, that was all.

Cripple, his mouth moved on the word, and then he bit his lip the way he used to do when he first started physical therapy and it hurt.

"Christ," Brady muttered to himself, "I'll practically be doing him a favor..."

"It's okay, Joey," I began.

Brady whirled in sudden fury, his balled fist flying out and connecting with my cheekbone. "I said shut up!" he screamed. "When will you people learn to do what I tell you, huh? Shut up, shut up!"

He hustled over to Joey and kicked him in the ribs. "I don't want you two together," he fumed as he stomped back to the table. "Not until I'm ready to do it. Come on."

He waved the small pistol at me and then at the door. With a last glance at Joey I moved where he motioned. Joey had a funny look on his face but I didn't dare say anything to him in case it might set Brady off again.

In the hall I felt my way along to keep from bumping into the heavy old bookcases until Brady shoved me sideways through another doorway.

Owen's bedroom looked like a monastery cell. Bed, chair, lamp... telephone. Also a window, looking out into the street.

"Sit," Brady said. I obeyed, while he picked up the phone and began dialing. In half an hour he reached two television stations, three radio stations, a reporter at the local newspaper, and the cops.

He told them all pretty much the same thing: if they wanted a really big story they'd better get over here fast because he'd already killed three people and he was going to kill three more, the final one being himself. He wanted them all outside within fifteen minutes, but if anyone tried to get in or if any tear gas or anything like that came in, he'd kill Joey and me immediately.

When he was finished we just sat there and waited until they all arrived, which they all did very shortly: squad cars and radio vans, the "Live at Eleven" action-cam truck, lights and wires, and people crowding and milling behind the hastily-established police line made of tape and yellow sawhorses.

Brady described it all with a kind of grim satisfaction as he peered between the slats of Owen's lowered venetian blinds.

"I'll bet they've got sharpshooters," he said. "What do you think, do you think they've got sharpshooters?"

I thought of Joey in the next room lying on the floor, very close to the windows and the outside wall.

"Yes, Brady," I told him, "I'm sure they have. Can I look?"

He frowned. "I guess. Don't try anything, though."

What they didn't have, apparently, was a plan. I didn't see Mike Malley anywhere around, but I did see two men in dark-blue windbreakers arguing by an unmarked car. One held a radio, the other waved a megaphone. The one with the radio waved at the house and shouted. The other one shouted something back. Behind them uniformed officers milled, waiting for someone to tell them what to do.

I was waiting for someone to tell me what to do, too, but it didn't look as if anyone was going to. No one but Brady, anyway, and I had a feeling I wouldn't like his suggestions.

"What are you going to do now?" I asked Brady. A moment's uncertainty flickered across his face before he straightened and sneered at me.

"You know what he *said*?" he demanded.

He was changing the subject because he didn't have an answer to my question, but that was just all right with me; if I could get him talking and keep him at it long enough I might have time to figure out an answer of my own, or the cops might too although I was not counting on this.

"He said," Brady answered himself, "I had no talent. So I had to shoot him, I didn't plan to but he just looked at me and lied."

Bell, he meant. Brady shook his head, remembering. "He just didn't want competition. He was afraid of me, that's what it was."

But not quite afraid enough, I thought. "How did you get him to meet with you again at all? And why my office?"

Brady's lips twisted. Outside, the megaphone sputtered to electronic life.

"Bell's suggestion," he said. "He said he was going to be there anyway when he was in town, he had to drop off some stuff he'd written for your magazine, that it was late. He wouldn't," Brady added bitterly, "be seen with me in public."

No, probably not. Likely he'd already suffered through a few of Brady's tantrums and didn't want to spark one in a bar or restaurant, and he knew if he let Brady into his hotel room he'd have a devil of a time getting him out again.

So: somewhere private, somewhere he could leave. It hadn't occurred to him that on a holiday I might not show up until after eleven, or maybe even not at all. Writers, after all, work every day. He got there, found the door open, and walked right in. And found Brady waiting for him.

"How'd you get inside?"

Brady shrugged. "Pounded on the downstairs door. Some guy came, a janitor, he was just leaving. I said where I was going, he let me in. Your door I popped with my penknife. That little lock you've got on there sucks, any fool could do it."

Down in the street the megaphone squawked and fell silent, as if the people in charge of it couldn't agree among themselves on what to say. Take a vote, I thought at them impatiently.

"Why aren't they calling me?" Brady complained, frowning at the phone. "They ought to call and interview me."

"I'm still not sure I understand," I said, trying to get him talking again. "If you didn't plan to kill him, when you saw I wasn't there why did you try to make it seem I was? Sort of luring him in, as if—"

Oops, wrong question. Something ugly moved behind Brady's eyes, something I really did not want to get riled up. Too bad, though: I already had.

"I didn't!" he screamed. "I didn't, I *didn't* mean to! But he laughed at me, he said I was a no-talent schmuck and I could take all the stuff I had, all the pictures of him drunk and out on the town, scarfing down expensive dinners and acting like some high mucky-muck big shot, and his wife with *this* jerk—" He waved an arm at Owen's room. "I told him I was taking it all to the *Enquirer* so everyone would know what a big fat snobby faker he was, him and his skinny whore wife, and no one would want to read his books anymore at all when they found out."

He smirked in recollected triumph but the smile quickly fell apart.

"And he said?" I inquired with caution.

"He told me to go ahead," Brady said disbelievingly.

From the street a few unintelligible words came honkingly in megaphon-ese. Then Brady's name came through very clearly.

Brady did not seem to hear it at all. But then, Brady's wheels were well off the pavement and spinning fast. Not much about the real world was getting through to him anymore.

"He said," Brady went on, "he had all my letters and they were crazy, and everybody knew famous people like him had to put up with loony-tunes like me."

His lip bulged. "He said he'd brought all my letters along just to show me he still had them, and if he ever complained to the police about them I could be put away."

More noise through the megaphone. I could not understand what the hell they all were doing out there, wasting time playing with the equipment while Brady's few remaining marbles bounced around.

"And then he laughed at me again, right in my face. So," Brady finished simply, as if it were the most natural thing in the world, "of course I had to shoot him."

Whereupon he hadn't had time to check out all the envelopes on my desk, one of which if Bell were to be believed was stuffed with the evidence of his obsession. So he had taken them all, and that was what a murderer had wanted with a week's worth of unsolicited *Pen and Pencil* manuscripts.

"But like I said, he was lying," Brady said. "My letters weren't there, just a lot of junk he'd written and other people had written. I burned it all."

"Brady," came the voice on the megaphone. "Brady, you are going to get a phone call now. Answer the phone when it rings, all right? It's very important."

"Can I check on Joey?" I asked, but Brady brushed me away.

"There they are," he said, "I knew they'd want interviews." Brightening like a kid on Christmas morning he put his hand out just as the telephone rang.

He listened a moment, forehead furrowing and lips wrinkling in rage. Then he yanked the phone out by its wire, snatched the blinds back and hurled it through the glass.

Bright shards sparkled for an instant against the black night sky, in the criss-crossed shafts of the police floodlights.

"The front door creaks," Brady yelled out as the blinds fell shut again. "Stairs, too. I can see the stairs from where I am, I'll hear you if you try coming in, I'll see you on the stairs and I'll kill both of them and all of you, do you hear me?"

He could see the stairs, too, I realized. It was why he had chosen this room. He stomped from the window and back again.

"I want live interviews, where are my interviews? I want a book reviewer from the *New York Times*!"

Then he seized my arm and what he said turned my blood into frigid slush. "They won't believe I really mean it until I show them something, I guess."

His laugh as he marched me toward the hall was hideous. "So I'll show them something. Come on, you're going to help me drag the crippled kid up to the other window."

"No, she's not," said Lieutenant Michael X. Malley from the doorway.

For an instant Brady froze, and in that instant Malley took the gun away from him, stepping forward and plucking it out of Brady's hand in one smooth professional motion.

"Jesus Christ," I said, staring at him. "You look awful."

Brady didn't say anything, just stood there with his mouth hanging open and the wink of Malley's .38 special police revolver twinkling merrily at him. He couldn't believe what was happening and it was taking his scrambled brain a moment to adjust to the awful new messages it was receiving.

"Goddam radio," Malley growled, keeping his unfriendly gaze fixed firmly on Brady. "Guy can't even go home sick, he's gotta hear stuff on the radio, make him go back to work."

There were cuts all over Malley's arms, hands, and face. His complexion was grey and big solid beads of sweat stood like pearls between the thin white strands of his receding hairline.

"Cute kid, here, nailed all the downstairs doors and windows shut. Couldn't nail the cellar window, though, could you?"

He took a deep breath. It looked as if it hurt him. "Are you all right?" I asked. "I could go down and get the—"

"G'wan, go get the goddam kid, I'll take this here birdbrain down," he replied impatiently. "You should've remembered, an old house like this always has back stairs," he told Brady.

I went past him in a rush. The room Joey still lay in was down the hall and on the right, and I had gotten halfway past the second door when I heard an unpleasant noise from behind me.

Malley was on the floor. In the shaft of light streaming out of Owen's room his face was pinched and terrible, both hands pressing hard against his chest as if he could force the pain out of it.

No gun. Brady had taken care of that. He stood over Malley with a bratty grin on his kisser and the .38 in his fist, while Malley lay there having the great-granddaddy of all heart attacks, helpless in the huge, crushing grip of it.

"Goddam stairs," Malley whispered softly to himself through gritted teeth, "made me feel short of breath."

His mouth had that bad blue shrivelled look I knew from some visits to the hospital with Solli. Seeing it I wanted to scream at the unfairness of it, but mostly I wanted to wash Mike Malley's creased face, hold his head in my arms and yell for an ambulance at the same time, because Mike Malley was a stubborn jerk, hardheaded and narrow-minded and just as disagreeable as the day was long, but he had gotten me out of some deep excrement in my life and I loved the stupid old flatfoot.

And now he was dying in front of me, and Brady had his gun.

Not even a hope the .22 might not do the job, now. You get hit with a .22, maybe you can crawl for help and maybe you can't. A .38, though, erases lots of maybe's; big calibers make big holes and you can die just from the shock, never mind any other damage.

"Brady Willamette," came the voice on that damned useless megaphone down in the street. Malley must have said how long it would take him and now they were getting anxious.

"Brady, we need to talk with you."

Right, I thought, and I need to talk with a cardiologist but I wasn't going to get my wish either, was I? On the floor twenty feet from me, Mike Malley groaned and rolled over.

"They want a show," Brady whispered, nudging Malley with his foot. "Come on, we'll give them a show."

He stepped past Malley's moaning body, now curled in a fetal position and caught up to me at the entrance to Owen's workroom. "Open that door," he ordered, "I'll bet they've got cameras right down there on the front step, now. We'll give 'em you first and then the crippled kid. Then we'll see who's so cute," he breathed, really into the big-time criminal persona he liked so much. "Then we'll see who's cute, when you two fall out."

I hesitated. Brady was behind me with that great big gun, and Joey was on the other side of that door, which was why I couldn't open it. Maybe Brady really was going to kill Joey, maybe Malley would gasp out his life at the top of Owen Strathmore's stairs. And maybe Brady was going to kill me too. But I wasn't going to open that door so he could start. I simply was not going to. So Brady stepped past me sneering and opened it himself.

What happened next happened so fast I couldn't even scream, but that was all right because Joey was screaming so loud himself he couldn't have heard me anyway.

"I am not a fucking cripple!" he bellowed, zipping past in a blur of aluminum wheels and a ferocious I-don't-care-if-I-die grin.

Brady took a startled step back as the chair's leg-rests hit him about three inches above his shins.

Joey motored forward, his freed hands—how the hell had he done that?—pumping the big wheels maniacally.

Brady staggered, arms pinwheeling, but at the head of the stairs he regained his balance with Joey still rocketing at him. Bracing himself Brady took a step forward, then a step back. And then Malley, who was lying within arm's reach, looked up blearily. Grabbing Brady's ankle, he gave it a vicious lift-and-twist. "You dimwit little moron deluded fuckhead," he grated out breathlessly as he did it.

"Yah!" Brady replied, toppling over the stair rail.

"...not a cripple, not a *cripple*," I heard Joey shout as his chair thump-bumped violently down the stairs, and I scrambled gasping after him.

When I got to the bottom he was on the floor, flat on his belly with Mike Malley's gun gripped very steadily in his fists. Brady was lying on his back about eight feet away from him, just now trying to shake his head and get up. The chair had flown by them both and lay overturned against the fern-stand by the front door, its wheels in the air, all four of them still spinning.

"Takes a licking," Joey said, "and keeps on ticking. I bit the goddam tape off."

On his face was a look I had never seen before, although I supposed his doctors and nurses and therapists at Weasels on Wheels had seen it while they were teaching him how to assemble and disassemble that wheelchair in double-quick emergency time. Probably, I thought, they had been seeing it for a long while. I was the one who had missed it.

"Charlotte," he said, leveling Mike Malley's weapon as if he had been handling it all his life, "can I stay out past midnight on the week-ends, do you think? Myron wants me to go with him to some concerts up in Springfield as soon as his mother stops grounding him."

It was all I could do not to fall on his neck and weep but Mike Malley was the sick one, upstairs on the floor with who knew how many breaths left in him before the oxygen tank arrived.

"Medic!" I yelled out the door, and slammed it again before some trigger-happy idiot could shoot me.

Then I fell on Joey's neck, while half a dozen grim-faced uniformed men fell on Brady Willamette who was already starting to sputter again.

"Important," he squeaked, whereupon a very large black man in one of the dark-blue police windbreakers began explaining to him just exactly how important he really was, and how if he moved a single goddam muscle the man in the windbreaker would have to take his head off immediately, right this very instant.

Brady, appearing to recognize the salience of this argument, tottered obediently out.

"You," I told Joey as the medics raced in past us, "can go anywhere you want to, any time you want to go there. You want me to set up your chair for you?"

Joey sighed, sprawled at the foot of the stairs like some sort of human pretzel. Smiling, he put his cheek up at me to be kissed. He was, I realized as I obliged, shaving three times a week now, maybe even four. Heaving himself up on his muscular arms, he gave a twist to his back and righted himself to begin hauling the more troublesome portions of his body toward the aluminum wheelchair.

"Charlotte," he said kindly. "I can do it for myself."

As it turned out of course he really could.

TEN

"I STILL DON'T get it," the typist said as she squared up the stack of a hundred and forty-four *Pen and Pencil* layout sheets.

Two days had passed since the events at Owen's house; only the amount of work we'd done in them made them feel like two years. They'd been long days for Mike Malley too, according to Solli who reported that Lieutenant Malley was flat on his back in the cardiac intensive care unit and not allowed any non-family visitors. But tests showed his heart attack hadn't been too serious despite the amount of pain he'd had, and since he was already demanding coffee and cigars—although not having these demands satisfied—and complaining bitterly about the low-salt, low-fat diet his doctor had put him on, the cautious consensus so far was that he was probably going to be all right.

Happily I watched the typist slide the layouts sheets off my kitchen table into the shipping envelope. With all her good articles plus one from David Fischer and one from Phileta Poole, plenty of pithily-answered letters from readers and a half-page display ad for the upcoming anthology, our new issue was stuffed full and fat as a Christmas goose, and getting in at least reasonably near its deadline, too.

"I don't see," she went on, "why Brady wanted you around all the time, or did all those silly things. Jumping you in Reggie Symonds's apartment building, for heaven's sake, tricking you back from the hotel—he should have just laid low and kept quiet."

"Yeah," said Myron Rosewater, reaching over my shoulder to pluck a cherry tomato from the salad I was making. "He was one dumb dude, all right."

"Myron," I said, "if you're going to stick your hands in the food I'd appreciate your washing them first. And when you have washed them, get some carrots out of the refrigerator and start peeling them for me, please."

Myron paused with the tomato halfway to his mouth. "Uh, how about I be in charge of the music, instead?" he suggested. "This cooking stuff is for the womenfolk—eatin' it's the man's job."

"The man's job," said Harry Lemon sternly as he came in still dressed in his hospital-issue green scrub suit, "is to do what the women tell him to do. Assuming," he added, "the man is lucky enough to have any women around to tell him to do it."

Myron chewed thoughtfully on the tomato as he headed for the sink. "I never," he said, "considered it that way before."

"Thank you, Harry," I said. "Why don't you go shower off the hospital germs, and then come back and do the garlic bread?"

"Hoist," Harry grumped, "by my own petard." Reaching into the refrigerator he pulled out the Almaden jug and poured himself a brimming jellyglassful; Harry's idea of heaven after a thirty-six hour on-call hospital stint was to stand under a pounding spray of scalding water while taking little ice-cold swallows of chablis. So he went off to indulge himself in this before beginning his kitchen duties, and I put the salad away and began slicing onions for the curry I was planning to make.

Out in the front room, Phileta Poole was teaching David Fischer to play canasta, Solli was putting the finishing touches on his vascular-surgery article, and Owen Strathmore was showing Joey how to make a quarter disappear, then reappear again as if by magic from behind his left ear.

"No, no," Phileta admonished David Fischer sweetly, "hearts are trump, remember?"

"Why don't you just let her stay?" I'd suggested to Philip Poole when I finally called him. "She shows no signs of wanting to run away, and she's been wonderfully helpful on the magazine."

Doubtfully, Poole had agreed; I got the feeling he was so used to having a wacky daughter, he didn't know how to handle a non-wacky one—not to mention one who had fallen completely and thoroughly in love with David Fischer. In fact, I thought as I glanced through to where she sat, the only way to get Phileta to leave David's side now would be to set off a cherry bomb under his chair.

Phileta hadn't escaped the care of her nurses in order to hire someone to kill Wesley Bell, or sold her earrings to pay for this service. She'd pawned them to pay for a single night alone in a nice hotel, where she did nothing more wicked than order up room service and luxuriate in a few hours of solitude.

And she hadn't feared David might be Wes Bell's killer for the simple reason that she hadn't known of any connection between the two; while the rest of the literary world had been buzzing over rumors of Bell's stealing Fischer's book Phileta had been too doped to the eyes to care.

Fischer had indeed been worried that he might be the killer's next victim, at least until he became reacquainted with Phileta, whereupon maintaining her continued and increasing happiness—not to mention her close proximity to himself—abruptly replaced any other concerns he might previously have had. Apparently he'd fallen for her as hard as she had for him, and at almost exactly the same moment, too, which I thought was really wonderfully convenient for both of them.

"But what," said the typist, "about Brady?"

I looked up through a veil of streaming tears from the onions I was cutting into pale white slices thin enough to read a newspaper through; they caramelize much better that way.

"He didn't jump me in Symonds's building," I said. "He tripped on a loose piece of staircarpet while he was trying to creep stealthily down the steps behind me, that's all. Aside from being nuts, Brady's other problem was that he was clumsy."

I dumped the onion slices into the hot fat hissing in the kettle. "He'd correctly identified me as the fly in his ointment—he knew from hanging around the police that I'd been involved with Mike Malley's cases before. And he knew that if I stayed involved in this one I could cause him a lot of trouble."

The onion slices began softening. "If Wes wouldn't do what he wanted Brady meant to knock him out, tie him up—Brady has an exaggerated notion of his own physical abilities—and force him to write praise for Brady's stories, at gunpoint. The police found Brady's letters under the desk blotter, by the way—I guess Brady lost his temper before Wes could show them to him, not that it would have helped. And like everyone but Wes, Brady didn't expect me to show up on a holiday.

"So the ink-bomb and the envelopes and the concrete block that killed the poet—they were all just to try to scare you?"

She paused with a strip of envelope-sealing tape in her hands. It had been her idea to dedicate the issue to the poet's memory, and to reprint his prized sonnet in a spot where my editorial column usually went. It looked, I thought, very nice there.

"Yes," I said, "Brady wasn't being kept such close tabs on as everybody thought. He'd learned to get away with things by making people think he was geeky and awkward, but harmless."

The onions smelled delicious. "Anyway," I went on, "he was in the attic of the office building getting ready to push the concrete block out the window, planning for it to just miss me, when it slipped out of his hands. That did it for the poet. In the confusion afterwards he managed to get away unnoticed. But Reggie Symonds's murder—well, by then Brady had lost more than his physical grip on things. He killed Reggie in cold blood simply to confuse me. It was only Brady's dumb luck that Owen showed up at Reggie's right afterwards, so Owen wound up looking even guiltier, and Brady's anxiety that made him lure me home from the Mount Washington.''

I turned the onions down to low and covered them. "He just couldn't stand not having me right where he could watch me—that was why he called Corinna Bell, too, to see if he could find me. The thing is, he thought I was getting a lot closer than I was.''

The typist sighed. "Like he thought he had some magical control over you, I guess. Knowledge is power, or something.''

"Or something,'' I agreed, thinking of Joey over whom I would have no power at all for the next seven days; the nationwide Wheelchair March on Washington to demand better public access for the handicapped along with an end to job discrimination began tomorrow, and would last until next Tuesday.

All the weasels on wheels from his advanced rehab class were going, he'd told me excitedly, along with two physical therapists, a nurse, and a board-certified orthopedic surgeon. He'd meant to ask me sooner but everything got all bollixed up with the murders and the magazine and all, and anyway, I needn't worry. The Econoline van they were using as a pace-car was loaded with sun-tan oil, Gatorade, fruit, and granola bars and a complete emergency kit for everything from bee-stings to broken bones—not of course that anyone was going to get any of these injuries. They would be staying in donated Holiday Inn rooms every night with all *kinds* of adult supervision and he had to go, he just absolutely *had* to go, so could he go?

And of course I'd had to say yes, although now I was having second thoughts. These, however, I did not get to express until after the curry was eaten, the dishes washed and put away, and the guests sent home. The place seemed empty without them and it was about to get emptier.

"You will," I told Joey as he packed happily for his trip, "be ridiculously careful."

"You got it," he said, pushing the frisbee to one side of his backpack to make room for a couple more science fiction novels, a camera with which he planned to record the whole trip, and all of his favorite Iron Maiden tapes.

I pulled a sweater from his top dresser drawer and handed it to him. Without comment he stuffed it also into the pack.

"And you will," I said, "remember to call me every single day, because if you don't I'll go nuts worrying about you."

He pulled his rain poncho from his closet. "You," he said, "are going to go nuts worrying about me anyway, so what's the point? But yes," he added quickly, seeing my look, "I will call you every day, just to keep you from hauling out the National Guard."

I sat down on his bed. His room with his telescope and coin collection, his posters and maps and his autographed picture of Steve "Steamin'" Clark playing live at the Pyromania concert, his bookcases full of science fiction and horror paperbacks and his rows of carefully-labeled cassette tapes—suddenly it all felt more like a museum to some distant, long-ago boyhood than like any real room where any real boy still really resided.

"And," I ventured hesitantly, "you will come back?"

Joey turned and grinned at me. "Sure, Charlotte, if I don't decide to bum around Europe for a year instead."

Then he saw the expression on my face and took pity on me.

"Look," he said, plucking something from his dresser-top and wheeling over, "you hang onto this for me, okay? It's an actual guitar pick that Steve Clark actually used, see?"

I accepted the guitar pick reverently.

"I'm not giving it to you, you know," he cautioned, "you're just holding it for me until next Tuesday."

"Okay." I looked down at the guitar pick, feeling much better since I knew Joey would never take off for Europe without his Steamin' Steve pick, and I was only holding it for him until Tuesday.

"Okay," I said again, "thanks." I settled back against his pillow to watch him finish packing, and he looked indulgently at me.

"Well, as long as you've gotten so comfortable," he drawled, "how about hearing my Latin verbs? I can't leave tomorrow until I get through one whole verb, or I can't start Greek next fall."

"Shoot," I said. "Oops, sorry. I mean recite."

"Okay, the verb is amare. It's easy, I think I've got it." He took a deep breath and so did I, reflecting that motherhood simply did not get much better than this.

"Amo, amas, amat," Joey began; "I love, you love, he loves."

"He, she, or it," I reminded him.

"Right, thanks." He stuffed his best old Jefferson Airplane t-shirt into the pack and zipped it.

"Amamus, amatis, amant," he ticked off, "amabo, amabis...."

"Amabit," I supplied. "He, she, or it will love."

"I know." He frowned. "I'm just wondering if I need these extra socks."

"You can always buy socks."

He nodded and tossed the socks back. "Amabimus, amabitis, amabunt. Maybe I should bring a water bottle. They say they're going to have them, but—"

He looked up. "Charlotte, are you listening to me?"

Out in the kitchen the refrigerator door creaked open as Solli went hunting for his late-night snack. You could set a clock by what goes on in this house, I thought.

"Of course I'm listening to you," I told Joey, not opening my eyes. "I'm always listening to you."

Brief pause. "Yeah. Gets on my nerves, too, sometimes, if you don't mind my saying so. I mean like really, Charlotte, a person watching you might get the idea that life was, like, really meaningful or something."

Deliberately he pronounced it "rilly" and I smiled. Joey's room was pleasant and I felt fortunate to be welcome there while he still lived in it.

"Anybody else want a curried beef sandwich on a hard roll with horseradish and mayonnaise?" Solli called from the kitchen.

My eyes snapped open, and I looked at Joey and he looked at me. "We do," the two of us called back hungrily together, and I scrambled from the bed and raced Joey for the door.

No contest, though. Somehow I'd already known that this time there wouldn't be. The glow from Joey's room spilled out into the hallway, but when I reached it he was already wheeling far ahead of me: pumping hard, rolling fast into a brighter light.

BARBARA PAUL
IN-LaWS aNd OUtLAWs

Gillian Clifford, once a Decker in-law, returns to the family fold to comfort Raymond's widow, Connie. Clearly, the family is worried. Who hates the Deckers enough to kill them?

And as the truth behind the murder becomes shockingly clear, Gillian realizes that once a Decker, always a Decker—a position she's discovering can be most precarious indeed.

NO DURESS

First Time in Paperback

MIRIAM BORGENICHT

A tragedy turns into a living nightmare when health counselor Linda Stewart's adopted infant daughter is legally reclaimed by the baby's natural teenage mother— and both are found dead two days later.

Linda's agonizing grief is channeled into a burning determination to solve these senseless murders. While suspicions of drug involvement might explain the sudden fortune the young mother had acquired, Linda's subtle probing takes a seedy turn into black-market adoptions.

"Borgenicht's perceptive comments on troubling social issues generate plenty of tension." —*Publishers Weekly*